PRAISE FOR
THERE MAY BE A CASTLE

'An outstanding book and a future classic' *The School Librarian*

'Mesmerising and overwhelming with emotion' *Booktrust*

'Not many books change readers' views of the world, this might be one of them' *Lovereading4Kids*

'Heartbreaking, surprising, uplifting – Mouse's snowbound journey is one you'll remember for a long, long time. *There May Be a Castle* proves that stories matter. They really do' *The Bookbag*

'Full marks ... for a story not afraid to take on some of the fundamentals of life while still managing to preserve the lightest of touches' *Books For Keeps*

'A gripping, memorable adventure which celebrates the power and scope of our imagination' *TheSchoolRun*

THERE MAY BE A CASTLE

PIERS TORDAY

Piers Torday

Quercus

QUERCUS CHILDREN'S BOOKS

First published in Great Britain in 2016 by Hodder and Stoughton
This paperback edition published in 2017

1 3 5 7 9 10 8 6 4 2

Text copyright © Piers Torday, 2016
Illustration copyright © Rob Biddulph, 2016

A CIP catalogue record for this book is available from
the British Library.

ISBN 978 1 78429 274 4

Printed and bound in Great Britain by Clays Ltd, St Ives plc

The paper and board used in this book are made from
wood from responsible sources.

Quercus Children's Books
An imprint of Hachette Children's Group
Part of Hodder and Stoughton
Carmelite House
50 Victoria Embankment
London EC4Y 0DZ

An Hachette UK Company
www.hachette.co.uk
www.hachettechildrens.co.uk

Mouse Mallory didn't like Christmas.

There, he'd said it. Or rather, *thought* it, because Mouse Mallory was more a thinker than a talker. (Or, as everyone else called him, a daydreamer.) Yes, he decided, I am eleven years old and I don't like Christmas – even if it *was* Christmas Eve. And even if his mum *was* going crazy trying to get him and his two sisters ready for their annual festive trip to her parents, over on the other side of the hills.

'Mouse!' Mrs Mallory's voice sailed down the stairs after her, along with different-coloured socks flying off the pile of laundry in her arms. 'I really hope that when I come back up you aren't just going to be standing there, and that your bag will be packed! We leave in one hour. *One* hour.'

Mouse stayed exactly where he was, on the landing,

1

clutching his rucksack. He peered inside. It might look unpacked to some people. But Mouse could see, right at the bottom, the only thing he ever needed to take anywhere: his toy horse, Nonky.

Even if everyone did say he was too old to be carrying toy horses around.

'Do you really need that?' his mum would complain. 'I've washed it a thousand times and it still stinks of trainers. You're too grown-up to be playing with a babyish toy like that.'

'You're such a *little* boy sometimes,' his big sister Violet would often add.

It's true – he was a little boy. His dad was stout, his mum wasn't very tall and Mouse was . . . well, rather small. In fact, he was the smallest in his year. That was why Albert Thomas Mallory was known universally as Mouse.

'So small, and so full of questions, like a curious little mouse,' his dad used to say when he was younger. Mouse had never been short of a question, that's for sure. Why is the sky blue? What does that button do? Will I ever get bigger? Not even his doctor could answer the last one for sure.

Maybe he would always be shorter than everyone else.

This left him with so many worries about the future.

Such as, would he ever be tall enough to go on the biggest roller coaster in the world?

But Mouse knew Violet didn't just mean that.

She meant that he acted little as well. He was eleven and apparently that meant he had to read books that had more words than pictures, or even no pictures. He was supposed to be able to sleep with the lights off, and everyone said he was too old to carry a stuffed toy around with him all the time.

Mouse didn't get what the problem was.

It wasn't as if Nonky was like the toys Esme still played with. He didn't play a lullaby if you pulled a string and he definitely didn't get chewed at night. (Any more.) Nonky had been a present from his dad – quite a long time ago, but not that long ago. Once he had been a fighting horse with a mounted knight, but his rider had since departed to the Giant Toy Crate in the Sky, and he was also missing an eye.

When his dad gave him Nonky, Mouse was too young to tell the difference between a horse and a donkey. He also couldn't pronounce 'donkey' – so 'Nonky' it had been from the get-go, and Nonky it had stayed.

Unlike Dad, Nonky hadn't run off to Florida with a software developer he met online called Carla. Mouse hoped she appreciated his terrible songs and corny jokes. He was surprised at how much he actually missed them.

But Nonky didn't force those on him either. Nonky never yelled when he was late for school and never sulked when he didn't want to play with him. Nonky smelt of the past and the good old days. He was soft, machine washable and made Mouse feel safe.

He was special.

And what else, really, did Mouse need to take with him? (Apart from some clean pants, and his mum was bound to pack those anyway.)

'Mum's going to kill you,' said Violet – who was much taller than him, even though she was only a year and a half older – leaning against the doorway opposite.

'Why?'

'Because you're always daydreaming and never ready on time,' said Violet. 'She's going to skin you alive, and then boil you—' She swerved out of the way just in time to avoid the rucksack being swung in her direction. 'Didn't you check the weather on your phone? There's more snow coming in, and ice too . . . so she wants to make it across the hills before it gets dark.' She clapped her hands. 'It's Christmas, Mouse!'

Mouse muttered into his jumper, not looking at her. 'I hate Christmas.'

'What? This is new. Give me one good reason to hate Christmas.'

Mouse kept his voice and words fixed on the floor. 'Presents,' he said.

Violet stared at him in disbelief. 'Don't talk rubbish! Everyone likes presents.'

He shrugged. 'Not if they're all stupid books.'

Last Christmas his grandfather had given him a copy of *Alice in Wonderland* and *The Tales of King Arthur*. Boring, bound in leather and with no pictures on the cover.

'To help you start a library,' he had said hopefully, peering over his glasses.

But Mouse thought starting a library sounded too much like hard work. There was clearing a site and laying concrete foundations for starters, not to mention lugging heavy boxes of books about. And having to be quiet *all* the time.

He had slogged through the books from Gramps anyhow, which smelt of old furniture drawers and glue. At least the pictures inside were good, especially the ones of the strange creatures Alice met down the rabbit hole or the knights in armour fighting battles. Still, there weren't enough of them, or any animations like in an app or a game. And what was the point of a book without pictures or animations?

'You only don't like books because you're a boy,' said

Violet. 'It's not your fault nature designed you without a reading brain, unlike girls. It does unfortunately mean that I will get to be prime minister one day while you will only be allowed to drive my car.'

Before Mouse could respond, Esme trundled across the landing in front of him on her trike. Clasped between her knees was the shredded remains of a stale chocolate egg, the rest of which was smeared over her face and hands.

'Choclit,' said Esme. 'Easta,' she added, just in case she hadn't made herself clear.

'No,' said Mouse, '*Christmas*. Christmas Eve. Look.'

He pointed to the gabled window behind them. Shimmering icicles, as sharp as prehistoric spears, twisted down from the eaves outside. From time to time a tip dropped off with an alarming crack. The fresh snow seemed to make everything quieter and louder at the same time. A robin strutted on the frosted sill beneath the icy spears, oblivious to the danger dangling above his head.

The snow carpeted the flat roof of the kitchen below, dotted the rails of the climbing frame in the garden and caked so much of the shed that it almost disappeared from view. For the rest of the year, East Burn didn't look like much: an old farmhouse on the edge of the moors. Today it looked like even less – just another block of white in a land of white. In fact, if you had been flying overhead, you might have missed it completely.

As if it wasn't even there at all.

Mouse watched Esme look at the icicles. She looked at the snow. She looked at the robin, which made her smile. And finally she turned back to Mouse. 'Easta,' she declared, and cycled off into the next room, leaving a trail of chocolate behind her. The robin stared at the crumbs through the window and tapped his beak against the glass greedily.

Mouse shook his head at the world outside. 'Snow,' he said. 'That's another reason to hate Christmas.'

'But this is the first white Christmas in five years!' exploded Violet.

'So? It doesn't make sense. When there's no snow, everyone says it's climate change. But when there is snow, like this year, everyone says it's—'

'Climate change.'

'See? They can't have it both ways.'

'What about snowmen? Sledging?'

'I'm not like you. I'm not good at any of that stuff. Making things, sport . . . I'm only little.'

'You can't use that as an excuse for everything, Mouse Mallory. Don't you even like going for a walk in the snow?'

He snorted. 'Like the one we'll have to go on after lunch

7

tomorrow with Granny and Gramps? That's not a walk, that's a route march.' Mouse began a mental to-do list: 1. Find out if the United Nations has a policy on forced marches after Christmas lunch.

'You think you can get away with anything because you're so cute, don't you?' said Violet, grabbing Mouse in a headlock and mussing his hair.

'Gerroff!' he said, flushing and wriggling free. 'No, I don't.'

'Yes, you do, and one day even you are going to have to grow up,' she said, closing her door on him.

He shrugged. There were so many good reasons not to like Christmas, like the teachers at school wearing tinsel over their ties, or, even worse, Christmas jumpers. As if they were Santa's little helpers, when they were still in fact *teachers*.

It was just pretend and make-believe.

That thought made Mouse feel uncomfortable. His chest tightened, his cheeks flushed and his hands clenched into fists. Because he remembered something that made him rage inside.

The kind of rage that isn't fixed by shiny wrapping paper or a toy reindeer with a glowing nose dancing to a disco beat.

It was the real reason why he didn't like Christmas.

Belinda Mallory was not a big woman, but she was a strong one. This meant she could effortlessly uproot her small son from the landing and deposit him in the Nuclear Waste Contamination Zone, otherwise known as his bedroom.

Mouse stood there in a daze, unable to stop thinking about the thing that made him sad. His mother wasn't in the least bit sad.

She was *furious*.

'Do you have any concept of what the word *help* means, Mouse?' she said, as she located the only known pair of clean pants in existence at that moment and stuffed them into his rucksack.

Mouse knew full well what help meant. Sometimes he would haul bags of shopping in from the car. 'Thanks, Mouse, that's very helpful,' his mother would say. Although sometimes being helpful was not a good thing. Like when he had given Esme too many sweets on Halloween and she had made an orangey pool of sick all over the lounge carpet. 'Thanks, Mouse, that was really helpful,' his mother had sighed, scrubbing hard at the floor. It was funny how 'really' helpful seemed to be less appreciated than 'very'.

'Mum! It's snowing again!' said a voice from the landing.

Mouse's mother glanced up at the small window in his bedroom, at the soft white splodges falling against the glass, and pursed her lips. 'Thank you, Violet, I can see that!' she muttered, zipping up the bag and thrusting it into her son's arms. 'Downstairs. Five minutes. Final warning.'

Five minutes later, Mouse was still standing among the debris of his bedroom, staring into space. His mind was far away, as ever. He wasn't quite sure what he was thinking of, but it was something to do with the meaning of help, the pointlessness of Christmas and what it would feel like to be eaten by a polar bear.

Approximately seven minutes later, Mouse was shivering on the steps outside East Burn, his ears ringing from his mother's latest outburst – delivered at very close range.

'I hate having to shout like that,' she said, struggling past him with a bin liner crammed with hastily wrapped presents. 'Must you be in your own world *all* the time?'

'No,' he lied.

'In our class, Miss Wilkinson gives us five minutes each morning for daydreaming,' said Violet, standing next to him, her favourite camouflage holdall in her hand. 'She says we all need to find our creative inner voice, which is more important than any exam.'

'Yes, well, Miss Wilkinson doesn't have to drive three children and a carful of presents across the moors by teatime in a blizzard, does she? I know it's not ideal, but we did promise Granny and Gramps we'd be there for tea.' Mrs Mallory slammed the boot of their SUV shut and dusted her hands dry of snow. 'We haven't got far to go, but I will need to concentrate in this weather. So if everyone could keep all outer and inner voices to themselves till we get there, I'd be most grateful.'

'But my inner voice today is Gráinne O'Malley,' said Violet.

'Whitty who-whatty?'

'Gráinne O'Malley, the pirate queen, Mum! We did her for a special library project. She was the terror of the seas nearly five hundred years ago.'

Mrs Mallory glanced at Violet and gave a low groan. 'Oh no, Vi, not today. Seriously. I'm not in the mood.

You'll freeze to death in that.'

Mouse took a closer look at his sister. She was wearing a floppy black pirate hat, one of her dad's old dressing gowns and had a plastic lightsaber tucked into her belt. She pulled the weapon out and pressed it up against her brother's nose. 'Give me the gold, traitor, or I'll pillage your castle and steal all your bacon. Or . . . you could just let me sit in the front.'

'Hey, that's mine!' said Mouse, grabbing at the lightsaber.

'Pirates take what they want. That's why they're pirates,' Violet said with a grin, snatching it back.

'No one is sitting in the front, or being a pirate, till we get there,' said Mrs Mallory, plucking the plastic weapon from their grasp in a single, practised, swooping move worthy of any Jedi. 'The Christmas cake we all made together is going on the front seat, as I've already told you.' And with that she tossed the lightsaber into the footwell.

'Prepare to repel boarders!' said Violet, sweeping past her brother with a flick of her dressing gown.

His mum let out a short scream, nearly making Esme jump out of her arms.

'Mouse! *What* were you thinking?'

He frowned and looked down.

Somewhere in between breakfast, thinking about Christmas and being carried down here, he had forgotten to change out of his pyjamas. They were his favourite pyjamas too, featuring robots of all kinds. There were robots dancing and robots firing lasers. Robots covered in egg marks and robots covered in juice stains. He was, at least, wearing his wellies, even if the one on the left foot was a different colour to the one on the right.

'Oh, I give up,' she said. 'Just get in. You've got Nonky, haven't you?'

He sort of nodded. At least, he thought he nodded.

'Mouse! I'm not getting halfway across the moors in this weather and then turning around because you've forgotten that stupid toy. Have you got Nonky? Look me in the eyes, please.'

'Yes,' said Mouse. 'You packed him on top of my Minecraft pants. Mum, why does looking someone in the eyes make what you say truer?'

'I'll tell you later,' muttered his mum, not looking him in the eye. Then Mouse and Violet – now wearing warm coats at least – a baby sister still smeared in Easter egg and a Tupperware box of homemade Christmas cake were loaded into the car at great speed.

Mrs Mallory reversed down the short drive and out on to the empty road. Snow slapped against the windows, and before anyone could make a sound their mum had the

Christmas-songs album on shuffle. In her car seat next to Mouse, Esme rocked back and forth to the music, drawing pictures in the condensation on the glass with a toothbrush. 'Easta!' she said, as the car echoed with the sound of angels hallooing and bells ding-donging.

On his other side, Violet was reading a book. It was the kind Violet liked and he found boring. They never seemed to be about anything, just endless non-stories of children her age, at school, and whether or not they got on with each other. There were no dinosaurs or baddies. Nobody got killed. And what was the point of a story where that didn't happen?

'You'll understand one day,' said Violet, rolling her eyes and turning another page.

'Vi!' called her mum from the front, doing that thing only mums can do, half looking in the rear-view mirror, half looking at the road, one hand on the steering wheel, the other stopping the Christmas cake from sliding off the passenger seat. 'Don't read in the car, please; you know it makes you sick. Remember how wiggly the road gets.'

As if to prove her point, the car swerved on a patch of ice and the cake tin nearly tipped on the floor.

'No need to make it more wiggly than it is already,' said Violet.

'Again, not helpful,' said Mrs Mallory, eyeing the teetering Christmas cake with deep mistrust, but gripping the wheel firmly with both hands.

Mouse stared out of the window. Everything he recognised was disappearing in front of his eyes, blanked out by the blizzard. It was as if they were driving through nothing. And in a rush it came back to him. A thought, as clear and cold as the white drifts of snow that carpeted the valleys, as hard to the touch as the car floor beneath his toes.

Breaking the daydream, Violet nudged him. 'Go on, Mouse, tell Esme what Father Christmas is going to bring. She wants to know.' And she whispered in his ear, 'Dream something up. You're good at that.'

Mouse blinked. He was back in the car. The snow was getting thicker. Everything was white and soft. The angels were singing about stars or mangers. Esme was still shouting, 'Easta!' at the blotchy, melting flakes on the window.

'Nothing,' he said in a dull voice.

The baby girl stopped, and blinked.

'Nothink?' she said.

'Yes, Esme,' said Mouse, his eyes fierce. His baby sister flinched. To his surprise, a voice suddenly came up from Mouse's belly, like a fiery serpent, spitting out of his mouth. He might be small, but one day he would be a man, like his dad, except he wouldn't run away when things got difficult. More than anything else, he wanted to be bigger and a grown-up, and decided now would be a good time to start. 'Nothing. Father Christmas isn't real. Christmas isn't real. It's all stupid.'

He sat back and folded his arms, ignoring Esme's wails, Violet's punches and his mother's anger from the front of the car.

He didn't care any more.

Because he finally knew why he didn't like Christmas. It was like the world outside the windows, which was hidden under layers of snow. Everything looked blank and unreal. No more real, in fact, than the daydreams in which he spent most of his waking hours, living in a pretend world where he was bigger or older.

And daydreams were a complete waste of time, as everyone from his teacher Mr Stanmore to his mother kept telling him. He wasn't supposed to waste precious school time making stuff up; he was meant to learn actual facts and figures so he could get a proper job when he was older.

But if making stuff up was a waste of time, what was the point of Christmas? Magical stars in the sky, a baby born in a manger, a man who didn't even exist riding a theoretical sleigh across the sky to not drop presents down your chimney.

Christmas was the biggest annual collection of made-up daydreams in the whole world. You couldn't touch it, you couldn't count it, and you certainly couldn't explain it in a multiple-choice-exam answer.

Which officially, one hundred per cent, made it the most pointless thing ever.

The Mallorys had left their valley behind, and the car was winding over the ridge of hills that lay between them and their destination. Mouse couldn't remember when they had last seen another vehicle. Daylight was fading, as the winter sun dwindled to a weak puddle low above the horizon.

The massive sweep of the moors, reduced to huge featureless mounds by the snowfall, seemed to rise up from nowhere – with not a house or any sign of human life in sight. A familiar view now appeared almost unrecognisable. Here and there a solitary sheep raised a woolly snow-capped head in greeting as the car roared past. Everything outside felt very far away and very near at the same time. Mouse reached into the bag at his feet and found Nonky. He hugged him tight.

He could see his mum concentrating hard as she peered over the steering wheel. The snow was coming down really fast. How much longer was it going to last for?

'I can barely see where I'm going,' Mrs Mallory muttered to herself. She caught Mouse's eye in the rear-view mirror, and as if she had read his mind, switched over from the Christmas album to the travel news channel.

'. . . The Met Office has issued a severe weather warning for the following areas . . . Motorists are advised to stay at home unless strictly—'

She hurriedly flicked back to 'Good King Wenceslas', gathering his winter fuel. Mouse caught her eye in the mirror and she flashed him a smile. 'Don't worry!' she said. 'Not far to go now . . . I think. Let's have a sing-along to pass the time, shall we?'

'*Gathering winter fyooo-oo-elle!*' Violet and Mouse chorused obligingly, while an inky dusk fell outside, filling in the shadows, widening the cracks and blotting out the light. Darkness changed the shape of things. Trees hidden under blobs of white icing loomed into the headlights like giant snow monsters.

Mouse shivered and stopped singing. None of this looked right.

'Are we nearly there yet, Mum?' he asked, not for the first time.

'It is many leagues hence, my not so noble curious kin,' said Violet, in her best pirate-queen voice. 'For this king and queen we seek do live in a castle far and far away. A journey fraught with certain—'

'Come on, Mouse,' said Mrs Mallory. 'You know how far it is. You've done this journey plenty of times before. It's only the weather making it seem different.'

They had, every year since Mouse could remember in fact. It took long enough by car in these conditions, but at least they weren't walking – which was how they made the journey every summer, with a picnic. The longest walk ever, which always took all day, Esme snug in her papoose, Mouse protesting every step of the way, his parents trying to distract him by pointing out landmarks and making up silly stories about them.

Like the massive forest that Mum tricked them into walking through quickly by pretending it was haunted. Or the old lead-mine flue that Dad stopped them from playing in by claiming it was a well full of monsters, rather than polluted fumes. Each landmark signalled by a cairn – a small pile of stones that travellers before you had built to show the way. Even a tiny church and some cave or other – he had been tricked into walking miles only to find out that these so-called sights were just as boring close up as they were in the distance.

They could make up as many tall tales as they liked. Nothing changed the fact that by car, or by foot, his grandparents lived miles from civilisation. 'But why do they have to live in the backside of nowhere? They haven't even got Sky or broadband. It's like going back to the Middle Ages.'

'Language! Come on. Why don't you play with the magic tablet if you're bored?'

She passed him the battered but glowing screen. Almost immediately he and his sisters became lost in the soft blue glow that lit up their faces, like a magical treasure trove.

Because, Mouse reckoned, an iPad almost was magic, wasn't it? A spellbinding black mirror that floated in your hands and which, with one swipe, revealed to you the whole world. Pictures from underneath the ocean, videos of the planet from outer space. Every film ever made, every song ever recorded, every game ever designed, every book ever written. He could almost see Mr Stanmore's point. Who needed to make anything up, when it was all here in your hands, just waiting for you?

It was perhaps, second only to cheese Wotsits, the greatest human invention ever.

A tablet *was* better than a book, surely? Black words on a white page just didn't give the same feeling of zooming and swiping and tapping. Things happened constantly, making him feel happy and powerful and strong. And nothing made him feel happier than the app he had just pinged into life.

JUNIOR JOUST.

It arrived with a blast of trumpets, some olde-worlde harp music and a massive horse charging across the screen.

'Turn it down, please, Mouse. I'm trying to concentrate,' said his mum.

Mouse wasn't listening.

He was watching, for the eight-hundredth time, the intro animation – with more music and lots of waving flags and cheering crowds – followed by the actual game where knights his own age fought each other on horseback. Mouse could choose his horse, style of armour, and a lance, broadsword or mace as his weapon.

'Gimme! Gimme!' said Esme, wanting to join in, which her brother knew from experience was a bad idea. But he could also feel the warning stares from his mum and older sister. Failing to react to those was an even worse idea. He knew that from very bitter experience.

'OK, why don't you help me choose a knight?' said Mouse reluctantly.

Which was how his knight ended up dressed from head to toe in bright pink armour.

'Flowa!' said Esme.

'Esme!' said Mouse. 'He's a knight, not a flower. And knights don't wear pink.'

He reclaimed the magic tablet and began to joust with the Pink Knight anyway, but he kept getting knocked off his horse as soon as he got on it. He got hit in the helmet with a mace and suddenly it wasn't magic any more. It was just stupid animated pixels on a screen with annoying music. He wanted to pick the Pink Knight up by the scruff of his digital armour and yell at him.

But he couldn't. All he could do was Quit This Game and start another.

Esme started to tug at the iPad. 'Have go,' she said.

'No — this is a grown-up game,' said Mouse. 'For grown-ups.'

'Hardly,' said Violet, who was now only pretending to read her book. She hated ever having to admit her mum was right, but the words were indeed starting to float across the page and make her feel sick.

'Mum . . .' she started, in a tone of voice that everyone recognised.

Mouse shuffled across the seat from her as far as he could get.

'Not now, Vi,' said Mrs Mallory. 'I did warn you. We're right on top of the moors. There's no way I'm stopping here. I can't even tell where the road starts and the verge ends. What if we go into a ditch?' Then she glanced at her children's faces and added brightly, 'But don't worry, we won't! Why don't we play a car game?'

'I don't want to play a game. Feel sick!' said Violet. She glanced at her face in the window. She had actually gone green. She put a hand to her brow. 'Really sick,' she said.

'*I feel sick,*' mimicked Mouse, stabbing crossly at the Pink Knight with his finger. It was lucky computers couldn't feel things, he thought.

'Don't be unkind, Mouse,' said Mrs Mallory, gripping the steering wheel even tighter. He glanced at her reflection in the mirror. She looked worried. Oh well. Mum often looked worried about nothing.

'Can I go?' said Esme again, tugging at the magic tablet again. 'Can I go?'

Mouse groaned. 'OK. But just one joust and then I want it back.'

The car began to weave around, on snow that had compacted into slithery ice. It was as if the steering wheel had turned to jelly.

'Mum!' groaned Vi.

'Sorry,' said Mrs Mallory. 'It was just a bit of ice. I'll slow down. Everybody hold on tight!'

Meanwhile, as Esme hogged the iPad, Mouse looked for something else to occupy his attention. He rooted around in the rucksack at his feet and found something hard and plastic.

'Yesss!' he said.

Trex was a battery-powered plastic Tyrannosaurus rex. Like a dinosaur crossed with a robot, and what could be cooler? Mouse flicked the switch in Trex's belly and his long jointed tail snaked from side to side. His tiny claws flexed and his eyes flashed devil red, jaws gaping wide.

'Roaaar!' said Mouse, as he thrust the dino-robot towards his sister.

'What is it with boys and dinosaurs?' Violet said, grabbing his lightsaber off the floor to fend off the attack. 'They're extinct for starters. Maybe with luck boys might go the same way.'

'Roarr!' replied Mouse. 'Girls for lunch!'

'Actually don't mention lunch,' said Vi, as the car weaved again across the icy road. She dropped the lightsaber and put her hands to her mouth, taking long deep breaths.

Spotting the flashing dinosaur, Esme dropped the iPad as if it was on fire. 'I go!' she said, reaching out for Trex.

'Esme!' Mouse yelled, lifting him out of her reach. 'Never drop the iPad! You'll break it.'

'No fighting!' snapped Mrs Mallory, hunched over the wheel, peering through the white fog that swirled in the headlights.

But if anyone heard her, they didn't pay any attention. Esme was too busy lunging for Trex. Mouse was focused on keeping him out of her clutches. Violet was just trying to think of anything that wouldn't make her sick.

Then several things, none of them good, happened all at once.

Which is how accidents often happen.

This was the first thing that happened.

Distracted by all the shouting and grabbing going on behind her, Mrs Mallory didn't notice the orange light flashing on her dashboard, which was the black-ice warning, telling her to slow down even more in case of skidding.

At around the same time, Mouse accidentally jabbed his older sister in the eye with the tail of a plastic T. rex. It wasn't too serious, but it was just enough to make her lose control of her deep breathing. Which meant that very soon she was going to throw up.

'Mum! Stop the car, stop the car!' she cried.

Distracted by Violet, Mouse forgot about Esme. She lunged once more for the flashing toy. He yanked it out of reach again. Only he wasn't holding Trex as tightly as he thought. The dinosaur soared out of his grip, the first ever flying T. rex in recorded history, sailing right through the gap between the front seats.

The motorised lump of plastic clipped his mum's hand –

She flinched, letting go of the steering wheel for only a moment –

Esme started to cry, Violet began to be sick, and Trex continued to roar.

Instinctively Mouse unfastened his seat belt to reach between the seats to get his toy back –

'Mouse!' yelled his mother. 'Put your belt back on!'

Which is when the car really began to skid.

Round and round it spun, two thousand kilograms of precision engineering, satellite-navigation system, cake, toys, tablet and human beings, gyrating like a spinning top on a frozen pond. Unlike a toy top though, it didn't stop skidding after a few seconds. It skidded right across the road, over the snow-concealed verge and straight through the flimsy wire fence.

The car ploughed on through the fence, trailing wires and posts behind it. It really was only a moment, although it felt like an eternity to Mouse. The SUV spun and spun and spun, until finally it stopped – at what looked like the brow of a hill.

For the first time in the journey, everyone was reduced to silence.

Only the engine was making a sound – humming fit to burst, steam rising off the bonnet in panting clouds. Windscreen wipers wheezed from side to side. Snow kept on falling, caught in the glare of the headlights, as if nothing had happened.

Getting her breath back – her heart pumping, every nerve trembling – Mrs Mallory jammed the handbrake on as tight as she ever had and wiped a strand of hair off her face, which was plastered with sweat. She swallowed.

'Is everyone OK?' Her voice was wobblier than the fence they had just driven through.

Esme was still firmly in her car seat. Her mum leaned back and squeezed her knee to reassure her. Violet had been a tiny bit sick, but not as much as she feared. Her mother passed her some wet wipes from the glove compartment and she mopped herself up. By some miracle, the Christmas cake hadn't even fallen off the passenger seat.

Mouse sat between his sisters, clutching the magic tablet to his chest like a shield.

He was daydreaming again. Daydreaming harder than he ever had in his life. Daydreaming that this very scary experience was, in fact, the dream. And that in reality he was at home, tucked up between crisp dry sheets. Or that he was lying on a sofa watching telly, or submerged in a warm bath – anywhere, but this.

'Oh, Mouse—' began Mrs Mallory.

But she never finished her sentence. Because as she was speaking, Mouse – still holding the magic tablet in his other hand – tried to reach for Trex a second time. And as he did, something underneath the car gave a great groan, like an angry beast being released from its chains.

The car was not, in fact, resting on the brow of a hill. It was perching on a pile of hard-pressed snow, like the plank of a seesaw. By a miracle of physics, the dinosaur's tiny extra weight had just kept the car tipped towards the high ground, and not the slope of the hill. But as he was removed –

The pile of snow collapsed under the extra pressure with a flump –

The car was sliding and spinning and tipping.

The steel-and-glass crate rolled over and over.

BUMP and *BUMP* down the hill it went.

Everything flew about inside. Bags and presents and books –

SMASH!

Windows breaking, a cake exploding, a dinosaur growling and a lot of crying –

The windscreen shattered as the chassis twisted over and clipped a rock tip, peeking up through the sea of snow. The airbag popped out from the steering wheel with a *whoosh*.

Finally, crumpled and bent, the car slid down the steep valley side, like a giant sledge juddering out of control. With a small explosion of boiling water, steel and fuel, the Mallory

SUV piled into a stone wall at the bottom of the field. This wasn't flimsy like the fence at all. It was very well built and brought the car to a complete halt without so much as a shudder.

Everyone inside jolted sharply, apart from the unbelted Mouse, who shot through the small-boy-shaped hole where the windscreen had been, like a human catapult with only an iPad for protection, followed by a shower of toys and smashed Christmas cake.

Which is where his story *really* begins.

When Mouse woke up, he noticed two things.

First, how very *very* cold it was. And second, how very, very, *very* dark it was. He checked that his eyes were open, and they were. There were stars in the sky above, for one thing. So many, a bag of sparkling diamonds scattered over black velvet, more than he could ever remember seeing before. But there was no other light – none of that orange glow that normally hovered over the horizon, from distant city lights and street lamps. That was odd.

His face felt wet too. He touched his cheek, which was damp and sticky. Was it raining? Or still snowing perhaps. Had that woken him up?

Then something salty and wet slapped his face.

It was a tongue, a big fat one, slurping at his cheeks.

Something was trying to eat him. He wriggled away. The owner of the tongue backed off too, startled, thudding about in the snow.

'Ba-aa!' said the owner of the tongue, in an apologetic kind of a way.

It wasn't eating him. It was eating something off his face, something that looked and smelt like Christmas cake.

Mouse brushed the sticky crumbs away and carefully sat up. His neck was stiff and sore, but seemed to turn in both directions. He patted his arms and legs, like he'd seen his mother do to him and his sisters after a fall. They hurt, although not so much that he couldn't move them. Speaking of which, where were the rest of his family? His eyes slowly growing accustomed to the starlit gloom, he looked this way. He looked that way. There was no sign of them. No headlights, no engine noise, no sign of any car at all. He twisted right round and realised that in fact he couldn't see one other living creature, apart from the animal with the tongue.

It was a sheep, a huge one, with tufts of unkempt wool springing out in all directions. And silhouetted against the deep star-sprinkled night he could just make out two curling horns. He had never seen a sheep with such big horns before. He looked at the sheep, and the sheep looked at him. It took another step back, looking unsure about this new arrival in its field.

'Ba-aa!' it said, in a hello-little-boy kind of a way. Mouse wasn't sure if it was a ewe or a ram, and couldn't remember which kind had horns, but he decided she was a ewe. Either way, she looked primed to bolt at any moment, as sheep often do.

'Baa-aa to you too,' muttered Mouse, wiping the sheep slime off his face. The sheep took another few steps back, as if further shocked that the thing she had just tried to eat could speak.

'Baa-aa!' she said, in a totally amazed kind of a way.

'Can you say anything else?' asked Mouse. 'Can you talk?'

'Baa-aa!' said the sheep, shaking her head.

That was not good. Up until this point he had thought that perhaps he was daydreaming. But if he was dreaming, the sheep would have been able to talk. This was all too real. Freezing snow. A real, live, smelly sheep – who was now looking for something else to eat.

The others must be somewhere. Perhaps they had been rescued already and there just hadn't been room in the ambulance. But there were no other marks in the snow apart from the sheep's prints. And where was the car?

There wasn't even so much as a tyre track. He could just make out the little hoof marks circling and criss-crossing the white ground where he lay, as if the creature had been checking him out for some time while he was unconscious.

'Baa! Baa!' said the sheep, nodding and daring to step closer.

Mouse put his trembling hands to his chapped lips and tried to shout. His voice came out as a hoarse squeak. It still sent the sheep cantering off to the other end of the field. He shrugged and tried again.

'Mum!' he cried, his voice no stronger than before. 'Vi?'

The words echoed around the valley. Nothing came back. Even the sheep was quiet, as if listening with him. Every noise sounded so loud: his breath, his feet crunching in the snow as he groggily got to his feet, his heart thudding in his chest.

'Esme? Anyone?'

Despite the perishing cold, he started to sweat. Mouse clutched his hands to his temples. Nothing about this made sense. It did not compute. Taking deep, icy gasps of air, which burned the back of his throat, he tried to remember what had happened.

Suddenly it felt harder to remember than it normally did.

They had been driving – all of them, in the car. They were going to see ... somebody, for a reason. But something had happened ... He sank to his knees and tried to remember more. Images floated up into his mind at random. A magic tablet, Violet dressed as a pirate queen, Esme drawing pictures with a toothbrush, a smashed cake ... yet try as he might, he could not connect the pictures. When he thought harder and tried to remember more, all he saw was a grey fog, as if his memory hadn't rebooted properly.

If he couldn't rely on his mind, surely he could rely on his eyes. Perhaps he had been thrown from the car or hit his head and wandered off by mistake. He peered into the night. There were no other people to be seen, or even anywhere that looked like people might be. But the landscape did look similar to the moors they had been driving over. He remembered that at least: *moors*. Why were they driving over moors though? His mind was jumbled, growing more confused as the cold gripped his brain.

Who was he? Where was he? Why was he here?

The answers to these questions had been certainties a moment ago. But now ...

Mouse strained his eyes, looking for clues. He peered

up the hill, searching for the black line of the road. If only he could spot a lamp, a barrier or even a safety mirror, anything that might him help work out where he was. But there weren't any of those things. Not even a fence or wall. Maybe some headlights would come past and he could wave down the car and ask for help. As he squinted up the hill more closely he felt his gut swell with sickness and fear.

There weren't going to be any passing headlights, because –

There wasn't even a road.

Mouse began to panic. He wasn't looking carefully at things any more. He was whirling, unable to focus. Everywhere he looked, the world seemed the same but different.

There had been trees by the road before – he could still remember that. Just a few, their bare winter branches shivering in the cold. Now there was a whole forest. A black sea that spread all along the bottom of the valley, impenetrable and spiky, sucking out what light there was from the night-time sky.

He remembered that even moors had walls and fences in places. Here there seemed to be nothing but open land, woods and total darkness. No far-off headlight beams, curving around an invisible bend, or distant glow from a lonely farmhouse. Only the frozen crystals underfoot, glittering in the starlight.

No. No, this couldn't be right. Mouse started to call again, not caring that it hurt his throat.

'Hello? Is anyone there?' There were some specific names he should be calling. What were they again? 'Names?' he called out, but that didn't sound right. His words fell into a silence as long and deep as a tunnel to the centre of the earth. His breath puffed into the air.

He called again, louder, and louder still. He cupped his hands around his mouth and hollered. Running back and forth – although that was hard because the snow was so deep – and shouting as his feet plunged in and out of the drifts. The more his voice echoed back across to him from the silent trees, the more desperate he became.

Mouse began to feel dizzy and sat down with a bump in his own soft tracks. There was no sign of any other human life anywhere. Wherever he was, it wasn't a place he recognised. And he was there completely and utterly all by himself. Then he couldn't help it, he didn't want to, he knew that he wasn't meant to, that he should be brave and strong, but he was only eleven and the littlest in his year. He didn't want to be alone in a cold deserted place that made no sense.

He started to cry.

The tears fell wet and hot on to the snow, and somehow his own sobbing noises made him feel better for a moment. Then he felt something hard and warm butting his shoulder. Mouse wiped his nose on his sleeve, looked up and saw the sheep. She was no longer nibbling at frozen weeds on the other side of the field, but nudging him with her head.

'Baa,' she said, in a sweet-old-lady kind of a way, which straight away made him feel about ten times better.

He stroked her. Her wool wasn't soft, it was tough, and her horns were sharp. But her velvety muzzle was softer, she was alive and she was being pretty nice to him.

'I know you can't talk,' he snuffled, 'but do you mind if I pretend that you can?'

'Baa, baa, baa,' said the sheep, in a there-there kind of a way.

Mouse laughed, despite his tears. 'Baa. Is that all you can say? I'm going to call you Bar.'

'Baa,' echoed Bar in a that-could-grow-on-me kind of a way.

Mouse put his arms around her neck, which she didn't seem to like much, but she allowed just long enough for some feeling to return to his fingers. Her prickly fleece began to feel comforting after a while. He clutched the curls tight and rested his forehead against her flank. His eyelids drooped, and he was just beginning to relax – when she bolted. Like a sheep-powered rocket, she tore across the field in a cloud of wailing bleats, letting Mouse fall face down in the snow.

'Bar?' he said, brushing his face dry with his sleeve. His anorak felt much rougher than he remembered. He looked at it. His jacket sleeves appeared to be made of leather rather than quilted cotton. That was odd.

'Baa! Baa! Baa!' urged the sheep from the other side of the field, in a very-frightened-actually kind of a way. He felt everything in him tighten.

'What is it? Why are you being like that?'

The sheep just tilted her horned head. Not at him – at the forest behind them. And he noticed – although he couldn't figure out why – that the forest was beginning to feel familiar.

'Baa!' she squeaked in a be-very-very-afraid kind of a way.

Mouse felt an invisible weight push against his back – a change in the air pressure perhaps. The ends of his ears and the tips of his fingers began to tingle. At first he thought it was the cold.

Then he realised it wasn't the cold at all.

It was fear, as it slowly dawned upon him that someone – or something – was watching them from the woods.

If he knew anything, Mouse knew that a silent watcher in unknown dark woods behind you was not good. He wasn't brave enough to turn around, but he was brave enough to speak. 'Hello?' he said. 'Is . . . is someone there?'

At first no answer came back – only a low moan, which whistled softly through the trees. It could have been the wind . . . but it wasn't. Because the wind doesn't make a clanking noise, every time it moves its foot. The wind doesn't sound like it is dragging heavy chains over the earth. The wind doesn't slobber.

Still Mouse didn't turn around. Bar trotted towards him and huddled into his front, as if she was frightened. (To be fair, he thought, she was a sheep – so she was probably afraid of her own shadow – but she seemed particularly scared of the thing in the forest.)

'I'm not afraid,' Mouse lied. He clutched Bar's wool between his hands, kneading it for comfort, which she didn't seem to mind.

The thing in the woods hissed and gurgled. It might have been a laugh, but a very cruel and mean one if so. A laugh that grew closer with every clanking, dragging step. The invisible pressure against his back grew. And the bigger it grew, the more Mouse didn't want to turn around.

So instead he started to say happy words out loud to try and make himself feel better. 'Mum. Violet. Esme. Dad. iPad. Granny and Gramps . . . Mum. Violet.'

Those names felt good. Where had they come from? There wasn't time to wonder, because they hadn't scared the thing off. In fact it had just shuffled closer. Even without turning around, he could tell it was out of the woods now, because the clanking sounded clearer and cleaner, in the open air.

'Please,' said Mouse, even though he knew no one but the sheep and the laughing, clanking thing could hear, 'can someone help?'

'Oh for goodness sake, stop whining!' said another voice, from the darkness. 'You sound like a little boy.'

'But I am a little boy,' said Mouse, all muffled and soggy through his tears. He looked up. 'Violet?'

'Not exactly,' said the voice, and its owner stepped out of the shadows cast by the forest over the starlit snow. It was strange, because Mouse could have sworn there had been nothing there before. He had scoured every inch of this field. But he had asked for help, and help had come. A horse, steam curling from her nostrils. A huge beast that shimmered in the pale moonlight, because every inch of her saddle, bridle, strap and stirrups were embroidered with brightly coloured metal thread. The saddle skirt was covered in patterns and pictures: flowers, swords and saints. Here and there the leather straps were inlaid with rubies, emeralds and sapphires, which gleamed as the horse turned, her tail swishing behind her.

But the most amazing thing about this horse, thought Mouse, was that she only had one eye. The other was covered by an eyepatch, also glistening with gold and silver.

You couldn't make it up. Except here she was, right in front of him. What he could see of the saddle looked much more expensive than he remembered. The eyepatch hadn't been made of gold. And normally this horse was small enough to fit in a rucksack. Not fifteen times the size of

Mouse and clomping impatiently in the snow. But there was no mistaking the missing eye and the empty saddle.

'Nonky!' he said.

'Wait a second,' said Nonky casually, as if toy horses grew gigantic and talked every day of the week. 'Do I know you? Do you follow me on Instagram?'

'No . . . you're my toy horse. No one follows their toys on Instagram.'

'Oh well, if you're going to be like that,' said Nonky, 'I'll block you.'

'Don't block me, Nonky,' stammered Mouse. 'It's not my fault. It is a bit weird though. For a start, you can talk, you're much bigger, you're on Instagram and I didn't know you were a girl horse either.'

'Get over it,' said Nonky. 'And get on. We haven't got much time.'

He hesitated. His brain felt more frozen than his body.

'But don't I need a hat or something?'

'Yes,' said Nonky. 'That's why you're wearing one.' She jerked her muzzle at him. 'And the rest of it.'

For the first time Mouse looked at himself properly, at what he was wearing. It wasn't just an anorak with leather sleeves. His pyjama bottoms had been replaced by scratchy woollen stockings. He tried to put his hands in his pockets to keep them warm, but found they were full of crumbs for some reason, so hurriedly pulled them out again.

Underneath the jacket with leather sleeves he was wearing what looked like a long-sleeved T-shirt, made out of equally scratchy wool. The coat was tied tight around his waist with a strip of leather, and on his head – as Nonky had observed – was a padded cap, tied under his chin with string.

Slung round his chest was some kind of shield. It was thin, rectangular and caught the light like a mirror every time he moved. Peering down, he could see that on his feet were no longer wellies, but leather slippers with very long pointed toes. And staring at the ground, Mouse was astonished to see something else lying there – all on its own and just begging to be picked up.

A sword.

Well, perhaps more of a long dagger, but still –

He took it. The blade was long and thin and round, like a giant knitting needle. And it felt lighter than it looked, almost as if it was made of plastic and air rather than iron.

'What's this for?' he said.

'You're a knight. What do you think it's for? Picking your nose?'

Mouse felt the weight of the cold metal in his hands. 'But I don't know how to use it. What if I hurt myself?'

'So I would say your chances of winning Swordsman of the Year are limited.'

'Don't I even get a helmet or some armour or something? I'm only little.'

'We'll see about that. Let's see if you can even climb up on me first, little knight.'

Mouse sighed. Nothing about this was turning out to be either easy or fun. 'I used to hold you in one hand,' he said to her, but no one looked like they cared.

He tried to scramble on to Nonky's broad back, but fell off into the snow. So he tried again, and again. She was so massive, especially compared to him. He lay spreadeagled on the ground, wondering whether he had the energy to try once more.

'Baa-aa,' said the sheep, in a not-very-impressed kind of a way, as she lifted her head up from some frozen thistles she was munching on and wandered towards the pair.

'So I think the answer to the climbing-on question, to date, is a big fat no,' said Nonky, lowering herself to the ground so he could climb on more easily. 'Hold on,' she said, as she lurched back to her feet.

Mouse looked around. He was so high up!

'I mean, *really* hold on,' said Nonky, and they were off, galloping across the snow, the chill wind blasting Mouse's face, making his lips burn and his teeth chatter, but he didn't have time to mind, because he was so busy holding on.

'Whoa!' said Mouse, because that was what the computer-generated knights on Junior Joust said if you tried to make them race too fast. But Nonky didn't whoa. She ran to one end of the field, and turned around, running back to the other, till her helpless rider could feel the warmth of her flanks and the sweat slaking her mane.

'Baa-aa,' said the sheep, in a you-guys-are-crazy kind of a way, standing well back from the charger's hoofs.

'Nonky,' said Mouse, gasping for breath, 'can I ask you a question?'

'You can try, little knight,' said Nonky. 'But I'm a horse, not a search engine.'

'There's something I don't get.' In fact, right this

51

second, there were many things Mouse didn't get, too many to count. But Nonky didn't sound very open to questions, so he thought he'd begin with one and see how he got on. 'You know how you can talk?'

'Ye-ess,' said Nonky, as if her patience was already being tested.

'Well, how come the sheep can't talk?'

Nonky sighed. She tilted her head round, so the golden eyepatch caught the moonlight, and bared her heavy teeth. Suddenly she didn't feel like his toy at all. She felt like something very big, very alive and very tough. 'This is not *that* kind of a story,' she hissed.

This was in fact the first time anyone had mentioned to Mouse that he was in a story. Was this another of his daydreams? It couldn't be, because to be daydreaming you had to be somewhere boring first. And five minutes ago, he was –

Hang on.

That was strange. He was sure he knew exactly what had happened about five minutes ago. They were in a . . . Nope. It was a complete blank. He couldn't remember, but somehow he knew that what had happened was important. Mouse made a mental note to remember what it was when he next had a moment.

'What kind of story is it then? Are we in Narnia?'

'Been there,' said Nonky. 'Got the T-shirt.'

Mouse tried to picture a horse in a Narnia T-shirt. 'Is this a time-travel story, or . . . perhaps a thingy in the continuum?'

'Someone's been watching too much *Doctor Who.*'

'A fairy kingdom?'

'Does this look even one bit like the bottom of your garden? It isn't any of those kinds of stories.'

Mouse didn't understand. He knew from school that a story could either be: Adventure, Suspense, Mystery, Horror, Comedy, Real Life, Fictional, Diary, Romance, War, Historical, Mythical, Science Fiction and Fantasy.

(Or Guinea Pig. His friend Farouk had insisted he only wanted to write about his guinea pig, Yoda, so the teacher had allowed Guinea Pig as a category.)

So this story had to be one of those, according to Mr Stanmore, or it wasn't a proper story.

Although it probably wasn't a Guinea Pig story.

Nonky looked around them at the woods of the valleys, silent and dark. She looked at their tracks criss-crossing the blank white field in uneven lines. Finally she gazed up at the endless galaxies above their heads.

'This, little knight,' said the horse quietly, 'is the most

exciting story you will ever be in. This is a story of peril, of quests and a brave hero. It is a story of magic and wonder. There will be monsters. Not to mention a king and a wizard or two. Prepare for fights, feasts, dancing and song. Strap on your armour and polish your shield. Blood may be spilt, battles will be won and lost, but with any luck our enemy will be vanquished – because this, Mouse Mallory, is *your* story.'

Mouse swallowed. 'And who . . . is this enemy?'

Nonky turned back towards the woods, which were twisted and full of shadows. And as she did, Mouse realised he did know where they were. It wasn't just any old scary forest. It was *the* Haunted Forest. But how did he know that, and why was it haunted? There wasn't time to think.

'Him,' said the horse. 'He's the enemy.'

Mouse turned to follow her gaze, but she snapped, 'No looking! Don't turn around. You must never look at him.'

He was too dazed and scared to ask her why, but he didn't turn around. He listened instead, to the thing that came from the shady depths of the Haunted Forest, stirring across the ground towards them.

Clank . . . Clank . . .

It sounded big and slow.

'What does he want?' said Mouse in a small voice

from under his padded cap.

'All these questions! He wants to kill you of course.'

'Kill us?! Why?'

'Not *us*, little knight,' corrected Nonky. 'Just you.'

'Baa-aaaargh!' said Bar, in a yikes-let's-get-outta-here kind of a way, cowering behind the horse and her rider.

'Can you stop him?' said Mouse, wanting to hide behind something too. The thing was getting closer, he could tell. It smelt bad: rotten and sweet at the same time. But he was on a horse in the middle of a valley in the moors, with only a padded coat, shiny shield and skinny dagger for protection. There was nowhere to hide. Once upon a time he would have hidden behind some people. What were they called again?

'No, I can't,' said Nonky. 'But . . . you can.'

'How?'

The clanking, smelling thing was nearly upon them.

'Why, by finding the castle before he does of course.'

Mouse looked ahead. He could see nothing but deserted arctic moors, scattered with colossal slabs of rock, skirted by miles of impenetrable forest, stretching out under the wide, empty sky as far as the eye could see. He knew his questions were annoying the horse. But he couldn't help it. There were so many. And he had to ask this one. 'Is there a castle?' he asked.

The horse seemed to flinch underneath him, as if he had wounded her. She sighed, her head sank low and then with a snort she straightened up again, although her voice wavered.

'There may be, little knight,' said Nonky. 'There may be a castle.'

And Mouse didn't quite know why, but when he heard this he leaned down and hugged the black horse tight.

At the bottom of the field, in the car, Violet came to her senses. And she didn't like what she sensed, not one bit. Her German-designed seat belt had kept her firmly strapped to her seat as the SUV rolled and smashed down the snowy slope. But the whole car, including the seat, was now the wrong way up, and as a result, so was Violet.

She opened her eyes and groaned.

Nothing was in the right place, including her.

The car felt smaller somehow, as if it had been shrunk. Everything felt closer than it should: the roof, the doors, and the back of her mum's seat. Wriggling her left arm out from under her back, which was hard because every pore of it stung with pins and needles from being trapped, she touched the crumpled metal door.

The car hadn't shrunk exactly, but it had been compressed, crushed in a giant SUV-crushing fist.

'Mum?' she called out, her voice echoing in the wreck.

There was no reply.

'Mouse? Esme?'

Perhaps they were still asleep, like she must have been.

Violet looked down, to see if she could spot them, but found herself only looking down at her pirate-queen costume. Or rather, she found herself looking up at her pirate-queen costume, whose dressing-gown belt was dangling in her face. It blocked what little vision she had in the dark and felt very uncomfortable.

But at least she was alive. She was breathing, and nothing – so far – seemed to hurt very much.

She tried to unfasten the seat belt trapping her, planning to gently let herself down to the ceiling of the car, which was now the floor. Only the seat belt, which was usually the easiest thing in the world to click and unclick, was twisted and not working.

The more she tried, the less give the belt seemed to give.

If she could just wake the others up, they'd be able to help her. 'Mum?' she said again, in a louder, clearer voice.

There was still no reply. But she could hear something from the driver's seat in front of her. Still suspended the wrong way up, Violet tried to reach forward to where her mother had been sitting. It was too far, and it hurt to stretch more, because something sharp and metal was pressing into her from above. A jagged strip of car floor, like a metal stalactite, hung down and blocked her way.

She closed her eyes, took another deep breath, and stretched again – trying to avoid the razor-sharp spear. It was like squeezing through the hole in the fence behind school that led down to the rough trees and grass, which was much nicer to play in than the boring tarmac yard. You could always make yourself smaller for a moment if you really had to.

Violet tried once more, and with the tip of her finger she touched something Mum-like – maybe a chin, or a wrist? And it was warm. Mum was warm, and furthermore was making the sound she could hear – a kind of snoring. Not like she was sleeping exactly, more a funny rattling breathing through her nose. She was alive.

Then a hot liquid dripped on to Violet's finger.

A single drop.

She recoiled. She knew straight away what it was. Mum was alive, but bleeding.

'Mum?' she said again, in a smaller, quieter voice. The kind that knows no reply will be coming. Trying to keep her words

59

strong and steady, and the crack out of her voice, she called again for her younger brother.

Mouse. Her very favourite little boy – and there weren't too many of those.

'Mouse?' she said, looking around, although in her heart she already knew the answer to that question too. The car was still, with only the strange ticks and drips of the smashed engine coming in reply. She cleared her throat. 'Mouse! I'm not joking. Please.'

Silence.

Perhaps he had escaped somehow. Yes, escaped, not anything else. She couldn't even begin to think about Anything Else being a possibility – she refused to. He was her younger brother, the daydreaming little boy. Absorbed in his own world most of the time, rarely lifting a finger to help anyone, unless he absolutely had to.

Adorable but useless Mouse was now their only hope.

Her mind drifted up through the jagged hole of car floor above, into the cold night air, hovering with the snow clouds. Violet imagined her younger brother trudging across the frozen wastes. A little boy, perhaps further up the valley already, no doubt still clutching those babyish toys of his.

'Oh, Mouse,' she said to herself.

Mouse might be small. He might be annoying. But he was

her younger brother, and at this moment she missed him. They could have talked things through; he was old and big enough to help her. Snow was beginning to fall gently through the hole in the roof, wetting her cheek. She looked up and saw stars in the sky beyond.

Which left only Esme. Violet felt a tug in her throat, not wanting to call out in case she didn't get a reply from her either.

That was a first. She was actually frightened to say her own sister's name. But she did. Again and again, trying to make her weak voice as loud as it could be, which was hard when you felt like an icicle hanging from a seat belt.

At last – there was a little squeak from the corner of the car.

'Are you OK, Esme?' said Violet, her voice sounding more worried than she meant it to. She wondered how Mum managed to not sound worried about them when she was – and for the first time since waking up, Violet felt real despair.

Mum was unconscious and bleeding. Mouse was nowhere to be seen. She was on her own – nearly on her own. 'Are you all right, Esme?' she asked again.

Another whimper came in reply. Violet wanted more than ever to squeeze out of her car prison. She wriggled and struggled, reaching all around her for the seat-belt buckle again. Now it couldn't be found in the dark. Then it could be found but still stubbornly refused to release, no matter how hard she pressed and tugged.

Violet wanted to cry. She wanted to scream. She wanted someone to help. But there was no one else.

Christmas Eve. Every single person for miles around would be at home, wrapping a present in front of the fire perhaps, or talking loudly at a party. They certainly wouldn't be out for a stroll, not in this weather, at this time of night, on this day of the year. There was another squeak from the darkness.

'I'm coming, Esme!' she said. 'Hang on.'

Except she was the one doing the hanging, and looked set to be for some time. Her shoulders sank. The situation was hopeless. The weather, the location, the outlook, the timing – everything was absolutely *hopeless*.

But luckily for everyone else, Violet Margaret Mallory was anything but.

The great black horse reared up, pounding the air with her hoofs. Mouse would have been thrown clean off, had he not remembered just in time that 'Rein Skills' was one of his highest-scoring abilities in Junior Joust. So he held on tight, as he had learned to in the game.

Stamping about in the snow, Nonky kicked clouds of white powder in the clanking thing's face, before wheeling around and galloping up the slope. Mouse gripped the reins even tighter, thinking as hard as he could about a high score rather than the pain in his legs or the prospect of falling off.

They rode up the hill, far away from the Haunted Forest and its creature. Mouse tried to keep his eyes straight on the path ahead, but it kept winding and winding, like a ball of wool wrapped around the pale hillside. Up and up it wound, tighter and tighter, making him dizzy. Nonky strained and sweated, heaving herself and her rider up over slippery boulders and slopping through rust-coloured brooks that flowed down the hill under the ice.

As Nonky finally paused for breath at the top Mouse wondered where Bar had got to. Or more likely, what she had got to and how long it would take her to eat it. But the sheep came skipping up behind them, leaping from rock to tussock, all the while saying 'Baa-aa!' in a this-stuff-is-easy kind of a way.

She paused with the horse and her rider, bent down to take a huge mouthful of some spiky weed and then together they surveyed the view.

It was still dark, but the snow-covered dales looked hazy and endless in the moonlight, and you could almost drink the scene in, with deep, painful breaths, like swallowing gulps of icy ocean. For a moment Mouse felt more alive and stronger than he had since arriving in this strange land. But as they looked at the rolling forests and hills ahead, he heard it again.

Coming up the slope behind them, noisy step by noisy step. Wheezing and clanking, it came. Hissing and slobbering, it clambered and crawled. Its stench wafted ahead in poisonous curls, sweet and rotten in the back of Mouse's throat.

Perhaps he should just check that the thing hadn't got any closer . . .

'Rule number one!' said Nonky, as she felt him begin to twist in her golden saddle. 'No turning around! No peeking, no looking, no glancing. Don't look behind us, whatever you do.'

'Why? There's only one thing you can't look at and that's the sun. It makes you go blind.'

There was a very long silence in reply. Mouse immediately felt that he had done something or said something he shouldn't have. The sheep looked at her feet, and for a moment the only sound was of branches cracking under the weight of snow, echoing out across the hills like gunshots.

'OK, so I think we need to have a little chat about status,' said the horse eventually.

'What status?' said Mouse. 'You mean like Facebook?'

'No, I mean, when I tell you stuff you just do it. You don't question it – you certainly don't challenge me. I'm in charge around here.'

'Why? I'm riding you. You're my toy horse.'

'Only fifteen times bigger, and covered in armour. So—'

'Why though? Why can't I turn around? Why do I have to do everything you say? It's because I'm little, isn't it? It's not fair!' Mouse folded his arms and stuck out his bottom lip. He was so cross at the horse he couldn't speak – his own toy, treating him like a baby.

Then Nonky snapped: 'Get off me. Get off my back right this instant.'

'Why? I wasn't doing anything.'

'Off. Right now. Come on.'

Mouse groaned. 'You are the worst toy EVER! Mum was right. I should have thrown you away ages ago.' The horse didn't react, but she did suddenly feel very strong and very big underneath him. So, sighing, he climbed off.

'And no peeking over your shoulder!'

'I'm not!'

'Look at me. I mean it.'

Mouse looked up at the horse and her rolling one eye and her glittering eyepatch, and down at her powerful legs, her colossal hoofs. He shivered. But the horse's voice was soft.

'I know you think that this is some kind of game, little knight. I know that nothing makes sense to you unless it is some kind of game—'

'Not true!' he muttered. 'And I won't always be little, you know.'

'Let me finish. I know that you would like this to be a game. Goodness knows I wish it were. But you have to listen to me, Mouse Mallory. Whether you like it or not, we are in my world now. So I implore you: *don't* turn around. If you look at . . . it, you make it bigger. And quicker.'

'Baa-ah-a,' said the sheep in an I-told-you-so kind of a way, her mouth still full of frozen weeds.

'I just want to know what it looks like.'

'You'll find out soon enough, when it catches us up.'

'But I don't want it to catch us up. You said we could escape if we found the castle.'

'*If* we find a castle. I said there *may be* a castle. I didn't promise anything.'

Mouse's back was tight, his knees were sore from rubbing against the jewel-encrusted saddle and his fingers burned with frostbite. He hated this more than anything he had ever done. And he hated Nonky for making him do it. She was the worst toy ever. He had kept her safe, stopped her from being thrown out and taken her with him everywhere, even when it had become embarrassing. She owed him big time.

Well, he was going to show her.

He was going to show her, the slobbering thing, and everyone else who had ever made fun of him for being little. Enough was enough. He was the owner, he was the knight and this was his quest. It was time to take charge.

Mouse put his hand over his brow and looked at the valley before them. It was like the moors they had been going through earlier . . . The view ahead was *like* one he knew, only so very different. These valleys felt deeper and sharper. There were more woods, and they looked blacker and wilder. The hilltops weren't so rough and round. There were no roads, no houses and no people.

Something about it felt familiar though. Perhaps he did know where he was after all. He had recognised the Haunted Forest, hadn't he? It was the home of that thing following them. What came next? He squeezed his eyes shut and tried to remember, but the cold was making everything so hard.

And it came to him – a distant memory of a summer walk. There was something else in the Haunted Forest, not just that thing. A small pile of pebbles . . . a cairn. Didn't some cairns mark a route? If he could just find the next one, perhaps he could work out the way.

But his frozen brain couldn't remember anything about

where the next one was, except that maybe it was down the hill rather than up. He thrust his hands in his pockets for warmth, and some more crumbs tumbled out, but he was too cold and tired to care any more. Mouse had to remind himself that he was not alone in the middle of a frozen wasteland just after dawn. He had a tetchy armoured horse and a friendly but not obviously useful sheep. He was in a story – that was all.

'I've got it,' he said. 'We need to find the next cairn on the way to the castle.'

'Which is where?'

He crossed his fingers behind his back. 'Down the hill. I think.'

'OK, Sir Google Maps, you got it,' said the horse.

With that, Nonky shook her bridle, so the golden bits clanked and the rings on her saddle skirt jangled and the diamond straps sparkled in the early-morning light. Mouse clambered back into her saddle, and together they plunged down the slope into the mist of the valley.

They zigzagged over dales and dells. They splashed through rivers of floating ice. They pushed through thickets and thorns. On and on they had to ride, for the clanking thing was never far behind. He felt the next cairn had to be near, if only he could remember *what* it was near.

The thing also zigged and zagged behind them, splashed through the same rivers and crushed the thickets to the ground. But it wasn't just the slobbering creature that Mouse had to think about. As they rode through a ragged copse, its trees sang with the hoots of owls, and the distant peaks echoed with the howls of wolves.

What's more, his sleepless night was beginning to catch up with him. He felt so tired that all he wanted to do was curl up and go to sleep somewhere. His eyes began to droop, and he slumped in the saddle.

'Don't do that!' said Nonky, but Mouse just slumped further forward.

'I'm not turning round,' mumbled the boy into his chest. 'You didn't say anything about not falling asleep.'

'Don't turn around *and* don't fall asleep,' said Nonky. 'Do I have to keep repeating myself? Two things you can't do. Two things you must never do, while we look for the castle.'

But Mouse was no longer listening. He started to snore. In reply, Nonky jerked at her reins, so that he jolted forward and woke with a start, rubbing his eyes. 'Where am I?'

'I'll give you a clue,' said the horse, skidding to a halt. 'It isn't exactly Fun Hall, Fun Town, Funland. Why don't you look for yourself?'

Mouse looked around him and shivered. Where was he again? He was on a horse, there was a sheep looking up at him with a worried sheep face and . . . there was someone singing, far off in the forest.

It was very faint, but it was definitely an actual human being singing, rather than an owl hooting or a wolf howling. And a human being might mean food or warmth. A human being might know where they could find the next cairn or even the castle itself.

'Come on, girl!' he said, pulling at the reins and kicking her flanks with his heels.

Nonky didn't budge.

Mouse grunted and groaned and kicked and pulled. But still the horse refused to move. 'Why won't you move, Nonky? Come on! I can hear someone singing. We need to go there. What are you waiting for?'

'You really never have ridden a horse before, have you?'

'Come on, girl!' urged Mouse again, flushed with excitement. 'I can hear someone. Just over there. They might know where the castle is!'

'Do you promise never to say *Come on, girl* again?'

'I promise,' groaned Mouse.

They soon discovered the source of the singing. Beyond the copse, in the middle of a broad plain, there was an old well, the circular stone wall covered in moss.

A well. Mouse smiled. It was strange this journey. He never quite knew what he was looking for, until he found it. Almost like he was making the whole thing up as he went along.

Yet there it was – just in front of the well! It was small, but definitely real, a tottering pyramid of pebbles and rocks: the cairn.

Either way, at least there was another person here. Sitting on the edge of the well was a man, picking at the strings of what looked like a miniature guitar. He was wearing similar clothes to Mouse, only his top was covered in psychedelic patterns of blue and pink. It was also filthy and full of holes. Fairground bunting dangled from his arms, and a drooping moustache dangled from his upper lip.

As soon as he saw the horse and her rider approach the man snapped into action, like they had tripped an invisible switch. He leaped off the well in a nimble bound and began to dance around them, strumming his lute and singing.

A knight so gallant and his steed came wandering ho
A knight so gallant and his steed came wandering ho
To seek the grail and win their glory-oh —

'Oh, great, a minstrel.' Nonky sighed. 'I hate minstrels.'

Ignoring her, Mouse said to the man with the drooping moustache, 'But we're not seeking the grail, we're looking for a castle. Do you know where it is? I think this is one of the cairns, but I can't remember what comes next.'

'Don't you worry, my son,' said the man. 'Leave it to me, leave it to me.' And he doffed his cap, tinkling the bells that hung from the tip. He stood there bowing, offering the cap to Mouse, who eventually realised he was meant to put his hand in it. Doing so, he pulled out a business card, which he read aloud.

'Sir Dragnet Derek, Professional Minstrel, Jester and General Tomfooler.'

'At your service, sunshine,' said Sir Dragnet Derek, flourishing his cap one more time. He spoke very quickly, without pausing for breath – *very* quickly. 'No occasion too large or small, Dragnet Derek Associates Ltd are proud to offer an unlimited bespoke songwriting and jest-making service for all – but not restricted thereunto by any means – coronations, uncoronations, betrothals, funerals, birthings, jousts, re-jousts, duels, gauntlet-throwings, spells, lifting of spells, abductions, rescues, escapes, unjust imprisonments and just imprisonments for the same fee, all deaths by means fair and foul including torture but I have to warn you I faint at the sight of blood and, last but not least, dragon slayings!'

He twanged his guitar and bowed once more, gasping for breath and trying not to let the pair see his red face.

'Dragon slayings?' said Mouse. '*Real* dragons?'

Dragnet put his grubby hand to his mouth, and whispered behind it. 'Word to the wise, sunshine, don't question the dragon's veracity – he don't take too kindly to it.'

'*The* dragon?' said Mouse, and he looked around him. It was getting cold again. He could feel the snow and ice creeping and cracking up behind him, as if it was sealing off any way out. But he didn't dare turn around. He had decided that Nonky was right. He didn't want to know what was pursuing them. As long as they never looked back, followed the cairns to the castle and got there before the clanking thing, everything would be all right.

Wouldn't it?

Besides, he was more worried about what was right in front of them. Because from the bottom of the well, echoing up from the dark and dank shaft, reverberating against the moss-covered stones, came a deafening roar.

He realised at last, with a shudder, exactly where they were.

It wasn't just any old well, was it? It was the well with monsters at the bottom. The Well of Doom, someone had joked, on a walk long ago. And echoing from far below was a roar that Mouse immediately knew could be made by only one monster.

75

Violet began to sweat, even in the cold, as she strained and pulled at the strap holding her upside down. The seconds and the minutes ticked by, and as they did, she felt more and more trapped. Awful thoughts rose and fell in her mind. She was never going to get out of here. They were trapped and would never be found. How long did they have before they all froze or starved to death? Was the car itself about to explode, like in the movies? Her heart began to race, making it hard to think straight at all.

And with that, like a cloud parting to reveal the moon, she remembered. What Miss Wilkinson said in their classes during daydreaming time. 'If you can't think straight, if you're distracted, or stressed – take a moment. Close your eyes, draw deep breaths and clear your mind. For a moment forget what's on your phone, what your parents said to you when they dropped you off and what lesson you're dreading most today. Let your mind float free.'

That was it. Violet couldn't *be* free. But she could let her mind float free, like she normally did when she was in the car. True, that was when the SUV was the right way up and moving, but still. She closed her eyes and began to breathe deeply. Her heart rate slowed, and her mind began to calm.

'Stay calm, Esme,' she said, and reminded herself to do the same.

She let her hand rest on the buckle, rather than trying to yank it. Instead of the nightmarish black thoughts that clawed at the edge of her imagination, trying to force the darkness in, she focused on good things that reassured her. Like the warm welcome still awaiting them at Granny and Gramps's, or the piles of presents sitting under the tree. The cosy bed in the guest room she would be sharing with Mouse and Esme. All of that was still going to happen, she told herself. It was.

The cord of her pirate costume tickled her nose again, and an even better picture came to mind.

Her pirate costume.

'Why didn't I think of that before?' she found herself wondering out loud, partly to comfort herself, partly in the hope that someone would actually reply.

Gráinne O'Malley, the real pirate queen. Violet had dressed for an adventure after all, and now she had one. It wasn't the kind she had been looking for – ideally she had been after a quest involving her rescuing a handsome but clueless knight, rather than a jammed seat belt and a car crash – but she knew enough about adventures from books to know that they chose you, not the other way round.

She remembered what she had learned from her library project about the real pirate queen, what she had endured and done. Violet had looked up Wikipedia articles about Gráinne and borrowed a big book on pirates from the school library. There was that clip of a documentary about her hero on YouTube, the notes Miss Wilkinson had made on the project and the coloured pieces of card with pictures they had stuck up on the classroom wall.

Miss Wilkinson had liked her project so much she had asked Violet to give a talk about it in assembly. She knew her teacher was paying her a compliment, but she really wished she hadn't. Not a wink of sleep the night before, her nerves jangling and her skin flushing as she stepped up on to the stage. But she had done it. And she had learned what she said by heart.

'Luckily for you, Esme,' she added out loud, 'because at

least it will pass the time. What do you think to that?'

There came a squeak in reply from the darkness, which could have been either *yes* or *no*, but it was enough. Violet adjusted her seat belt, cleared her throat and began to address her audience.

'Gráinne O'Malley started out as a pirate, but she was so successful that by the end of her career she owned a thousand cows and horses of her own. Even the non-pirate Queen of England at the time, Elizabeth I, respected her and invited her for tea, where she agreed to help her. This was unusual because not only was Gráinne a pirate, but Irish too, and the queen was always invading Ireland, so they weren't automatically going to be friends.'

Violet paused to catch her breath. It was hard, speaking in the cold. It didn't matter. Gráinne O'Malley – she had learned – was fierce, but also loyal and brave.

'She would have known what to do in this situation, Esme,' she said. 'If she was here, we could ask her.'

That was just it. Gráinne O'Malley wasn't here. She had died more than four hundred years ago.

But Violet did have the next best thing. She'd have been willing to bet there wasn't another living person within fifty miles who knew more about the pirate legend than she did.

'Once Gráinne had decided to do something, she never gave up. In fact her own name showed how determined she was. Her actual name was Grace, Grace O'Malley. Her father had refused to let her go to sea, because he thought her long hair would get trapped in the rigging. So she cut off all her hair, and everyone gave her a new Gaelic nickname of "Gráinne Mhaol" or "Bald Grace". Gráinne O'Malley, you see, Esme?'

She cut off her own beautiful red hair so she could follow her destiny.

Wait a minute.

Violet stopped reciting and looked up. Gráinne O'Malley might have died over four hundred years ago, but she could still help. As it happened, Violet wasn't trapped in the rigging by her hair, but by the rigging. And sticking right into the rigging — which in this case was a knot of seat belt and dressing-gown cord — was the thing she had been trying to carefully avoid.

The stalactite of car roof.

So she did the opposite. Leaning forward, pushing with all her weight, she managed to hook the seat-belt strap over the jagged strip of metal. And she started to sway. She swayed and she pulled, using her body to drag the belt back and forth across the sharp metal edge, again and again. But still nothing happened. It felt as if she would have to do this movement for the rest of her life.

In that case, Violet decided, dragging the fraying belt over the ripped metal yet again, for the rest of her life she would no longer be plain Violet Margaret Mallory. She was going to take control, and be tough, and fearless, and ruthless.

She was going to be the pirate queen, at least of this ship. She would be a pirate queen as famous for her dressing gown as Gráinne O'Malley was for her shorn head.

'I am Captain Violet O'Belty,' she declared, surprisingly loudly for someone hanging upside down. 'And I will be free!'

'Finally,' said Nonky, listening to the roars from deep below the ground. 'A dragon. Things are beginning to look up. If I could rub my hoofs with glee, I would.'

She made a move to peer down the well, but Mouse pulled at her reins, shouting, 'Whoa, Nonky! Whoa!' He jumped off. 'What are you doing? Are you crazy? Don't go near there! That dragon might be dangerous. It might want to kill us. Or even worse, eat us.'

'What kind of warrior are you exactly, little knight?' said Nonky, her eyepatch glinting more fiercely than ever.

'Yes, what kind of knight are you, sunshine?' said Dragnet, twisting the ends of his moustache and giving Mouse the once-over. 'Can't say I recognise your colours. Very unusual provenance, I'm sure.' He reached inside his

82

jerkin and pulled out a small book. It was called *Everything You Ever Wanted to Know About Knights Gallant But Never Dared Ask*. The minstrel thumbed through the browning pages, squinting at Mouse. 'Hmm. Sir Jacques the Jocular?'

Mouse shook his head. He was pretty sure he didn't know what Jocular meant, and even more sure he didn't feel like it. In fact he still felt half asleep, and wondered if anyone would notice if he dozed off again. Dragnet began to speak faster and faster. It was like he too was trying to keep Mouse awake.

'Sir Egbert the Egregious? Sir Balon the Bibulous? Sir Lister the L—'

'There is nothing funny about being little!' scowled Mouse from under his cap.

'I never said there was, sunshine. He's the finest knight there is, no two ways about it. Sir Gawain the Gawayward p'raps? Sir Peregrine Parsnip? Sir Tristan Tittle-Tattle? Sir Charmain the Chump?'

'You're just making them up now.'

'Nothing wrong with making stuff up, cheeky chops. It's what makes the world go round. Certainly this one,' said Dragnet, snapping the book shut. 'So who exactly are you, sunshine, if you don't mind my asking?'

'I am—' began Mouse, but to his surprise Nonky interrupted. He was glad she had, because the strange thing was, he couldn't quite remember. He knew he was someone who lived somewhere with some people. It had all been so clear before, and yet . . .

'Never mind who he is,' she said. 'Who's the dragon?'

'Who's the dragon? I thought you'd never ask.' Dragnet smiled, picking up his lute.

'Now I wish I hadn't,' said the horse.

And as they stood around the well, the roars echoing below, Dragnet placed his grimy slippered foot upon the crumbling wall and began to sing. As he did, some birds started up from a nearby bush in fright. His voice sounded like a rusty chain being pulled along a pipe lined with crushed glass, but he didn't seem to notice.

> *There are tales I could tell*
> *Of monsters and spooks*
> *Just like those found in books.*
> *But did I tell you yet*
> *About the worst-ever pet?*
> *He's got green scales with claws*
> *And fire-breathing jaws . . .*

Mouse wished he could press a button that would make him stop, like in a TV talent show. All he really wanted to do was sit down and have a nap. Sir Dragnet skipped round behind him and whispered the next verse in his ear, his whiskers tickling Mouse's neck.

> *Who's the dragon?*
> *That's the question*
> *With which I'm wrestling.*
> *There are yarns I could spin*
> *To make you leap out yer skin*
> *Of knights spreading gore*
> *Just like days gone of yore …*

It was strange. The song was awful, almost like the kind of song someone he once knew used to make up.

He began to see in his mind what the song was conjuring up. It was making him feel less sleepy. Nonky had closed her one eye, as if by not seeing the minstrel she could stop herself from hearing him too. Mouse looked around to see what the sheep thought, but she was nowhere to be seen. Where had she gone? Then he remembered. There had been heather, on the hilltop. Typical sheep.

Before he could worry about whether Bar would

find them again, Sir Dragnet was down on one knee, serenading him, his bony kneecap poking through the hole in his stocking.

> *But have I sung the ballad*
> *To make you choke on your salad*
> *Of dark wings in the sky*
> *A pointed tail in your eye?*
> *Who's the dragon? A terror for sure.*
> *Turn back home now, lock the door!*

The minstrel was leaping around now, his eyes shifting from side to side. He flung his head back and threw his arm into the air. One moment he was behind Nonky, the next he was popping up beyond the well. The music grew faster and faster, and Mouse began to be worried that he might see the creature in question appear at any second. At least it might stop the minstrel singing, if nothing else.

> *Who's the dragon? He's giant and green.*
> *You never saw a monster so mean.*
> *Who's the dragon? I don't really care.*
> *Just don't enter his lair.*
> *Who's the dragon? In our land medieval*

He's the king of pure evil.

I hope you like barbecue –

It's what he'll do to you.

Who's the dragon? One of his aims

Is to torch us with flames.

He's a brute, a terror, a psycho,

The death-and-pain maestro.

There are yarns I could spin

Of beasts and monsters and spooks

Just like the kind found in books.

But my time's nearly done

So for Pete's sake – just RUN!

Sir Dragnet stopped prancing around, abruptly packing his lute away, strapping it to his shoulder. He began gathering up the rest of his belongings – a tin cup, plate and tatty blanket – stuffing them into his patchwork sack, muttering to himself. Beads of sweat were dripping down his forehead from under his cap.

'Is that the end?' said Mouse, who thought it was a very weird way to finish a song. He stretched and yawned, blinking. At least it had woken him up – for the moment.

'It will be, if you don't look to it,' said Dragnet, and he jumped on to Nonky, his harlequin clothes looking very dishevelled against her sparkling gold-and-emerald saddle.

'Hey!' shouted Mouse. 'That's my horse.'

'*Was*,' said Dragnet. 'It *was* your horse.' And he pointed to the business card in Mouse's hands. With his dirty-nailed thumb he indicated the words in very small print at the bottom. 'All songs, jests, japes, ditties and fooleries provided by Dragnet Associates are to be paid for on delivery. We accept coins, bars of gold, silver nuggets, precious stones, dragon treasure and gifts from the gods. Warning: your horse may be at risk if you do not keep up payments on your ballad.'

'But I haven't got any gold or nuggets or whatever,' said Mouse. And even just the word *nuggets* made his stomach ache with hunger, so things were even worse than before.

'Sorry, kiddo,' said Nonky. 'I wish I made the rules in this town. But I don't. So sit tight, wrap up warm, say your prayers, and remember: whatever you do, don't turn around. Or fall asleep.'

Before Mouse could ask who did make the rules, Sir Dragnet cried, 'Tally-ho!' and, digging in his multicoloured heels, he and Nonky galloped off over the plain and out of sight. Mouse looked after them, wondering if the direction they had gone was the way to the castle. If only Bar was still here and not stuffing her face somewhere.

Suddenly he thought how nice it would be to hear a 'Baa' in a don't-worry-cheer-up-I'm sure-they'll-be-back-soon kind of a way. Anyone to keep him company. He was totally alone, without even a sheep – any friend would do.

That was funny though. What with no sheep, musician or horse, he would have expected the plain to be still and quiet again, only it wasn't. It was the opposite of quiet. There was a scratching noise that was making the Well of Doom very un-quiet. Scratching and dragging, grunting and roaring, as something hauled itself up the well shaft, making the sides shake and clouds of stone dust explode into the air.

Mouse didn't know what to do. He was alone in a strange and mysterious land, which only half made sense, and there was a monster – presumed dragon – that sounded the size of a high-speed train, clambering up a tunnel towards him.

So he did the only logical thing to do. He put his hand on his sword.

At first, though, Mouse had no idea what to actually do. He'd seen swords in movies and occasionally wielded one in Junior Joust, but how on earth did you use them in real life?

The ground started to shake. He felt himself bounce up and down, as the monster advancing from below struck the pit walls like a mallet striking a gong. Hairline cracks formed in the well rim and little pebbles tumbled off the top of the cairn.

A slow sense of dread stole over Mouse as he realised that he was going to have to sort this one out himself. He groaned. This meant thinking plans through, imagining a sequence of choices and consequences unfolding, and that always made his mind ache. Except there wasn't time to think anything through. He pulled his dagger from its belt and tried to swing it around like the lightsaber he had to fight Violet with in one of her daily pirate raids on his bedroom, but this seemed much heavier and harder to do. Everything seemed heavier and harder in this world.

Violet. He said her name. But who was she? Where was she? Not here, that's for sure.

Meanwhile, he couldn't yet see the monster. He could hear it though. A long, guttural growl, ripped from the centre of the earth itself. The fat sound rippled through the air, prickling each and every hair on the back of Mouse's neck. This was insane. A real dragon was coming. You couldn't make it up. He gripped the sword even tighter – and then lowered it again in disbelief.

A thought had hit him – like a dragon's clawed fist was probably just about to.

You couldn't make it up. But perhaps he was. This was his story – that was what Nonky had said. If it was, why was he inventing this dragon charging towards him? Did that mean he could also invent a way to defeat it?

A spark in his brain told him his sword should have a name. It seemed a bit silly, to name an inanimate object, but hadn't he read that in a book once, or seen it in a film? It didn't matter – a story of some kind anyhow. He racked his brain, but couldn't think of anything that sounded like a good name for a sword.

And it came to him. 'Keith.'

Keith? No one had ever killed a dragon with a sword called Keith, he was fairly sure of that.

Nigel Knife? Dennis Dagger? The Brian Blade? He winced. He'd had no idea it would be so difficult to come up with a cool sword name. Then he remembered something . . . He had been listening to music with someone. He remembered the word *Wenceslas*. That sounded good.

Mouse named his lightsaber Wenceslas.

Wait. It wasn't a lightsaber. It was a sword. An ancient magical sword, called *Wenceslas the Dragon Slayer*. That sounded even better. It sounded better for precisely thirty seconds, until the ground shook again and the well wall split in half.

Just like that. A massive great stone wall, cracked clean in half, like there had been a bomb or an earthquake. The ground bounced again, and so did Mouse. He took a step back, gripping Wenceslas so tight he feared his hands might snap. His face was rigid with terror at the thought of the creature about to emerge from the depths.

It was bigger and more frightening in the flesh than

Mouse could ever have imagined.

It also wasn't a dragon.

Because crawling out from the remains of the well, measuring six metres long at least, an oversized body on two gigantic chicken legs, with the sharpest teeth Mouse had ever seen, was a dinosaur.

A dinosaur, running around in a land of armoured horses and minstrels. That made literally *no* sense.

A Tyrannosaurus rex, to be precise, covered with dark scales fringing a tight pale belly. Its head was the size of a small car and his narrow eyes were flashing amber, like traffic lights on the blink. They coolly took in Mouse, while his pink tongue licked his chops. The jointed mechanical tail swept away the remains of the well with a single flick.

Mouse knew only one dinosaur with a jointed tail.

'No way,' said Mouse. 'Trex?'

Trex stopped stomping and swaying. He lurched, his giant head nosing in the boy's direction. Two jets of steam curled out of the nostril slits. The dinosaur opened his colossal jaws, strands of spit stretching between them, and roared. It was a foul, rotten-meat-stinking, throaty roar, which pressed Mouse's eyes into his skull and blew his hair back.

Trex began to charge, thumping at great speed across the ground towards him. He couldn't turn around, or go back the way he had come because of . . . the thing he wasn't allowed to look at. Whatever it was, somehow he just knew it was worse than a T. rex.

Much worse.

'Trex! It's me! Go away!' he shouted, but it was hard to hear his own voice above the bellowing and the thumping of the clawed feet. The monster's ridge of spikes sprang up sharp along his spine, and his stony bulk blocked out the sky. Mouse cowered in his approaching shadow, mesmerised by the creature's eyes, which glowed as if they were on fire. Close up, he could see that the teeth were filthy with dirt and blood, their points as sharp as spears.

With a gulp, Mouse realised that once you have seen teeth like that close up, it is likely they will be the last thing you ever see. He quickly worked out that he had three options:

1) Jump in the well.
2) Get eaten alive by a giant version of his own toy.
3) Hide behind what remained of the well.

Neither 1) nor 3) seemed to necessarily cancel out 2).

Everything began to feel very bad indeed.

'I can't do this,' he whimpered, trying hard to hold Wenceslas steady. He had hoped his sword was a dragon slayer. He had no idea if it was a dinosaur slayer. 'I can't do this. Mum, Vi, Esme. I'm sorry. I'm sorry—'

The names came back to him, briefly. He called and he cried out – for his mum, for his sisters, and for the giant living toy horse that had just been stolen by a minstrel.

The T. rex raised itself to its full height for one last roar and, leaning forward, sniffed the air. Mouse stood as still as he could, holding his breath. It had worked in *Jurassic Park*, hadn't it? The dinosaur snorted with derision, and Mouse remembered with a cold dread that *they had watched the film together*.

He had sat in front of the TV, playing with Trex. 'You see, Trex, if you ever tried to eat me, I would just keep very still, because your sense of movement is better than your sense of sight.' Mouse wished more than anything he hadn't done that now, as Trex tilted his head to one side, considering his prey.

Then, in one swift move, he stretched his jaws wide open and down over the boy.

'Are you OK, first mate?' said Captain Violet O'Belty, her voice sounding a bit stronger than before.

A definite squeak came in reply. The pirate queen wanted more than ever to squeeze out of the rigging that trapped her. She wriggled and struggled, sawing the rope over and over with the cutlass as hard as she could.

Violet wanted to cry. She wanted to scream. She wanted someone else to help and do this for her.

But she had learned over the years that sometimes you had to help yourself. That was what pirate queens did, a voice from the past whispered in her ear. She had learned this most keenly after Dad had left, and as the eldest child it was a lesson she always seemed to have to learn before everyone else. It wasn't fair, but – there – she had done it, and the seat belt jerked apart with a silent snap.

Violet tumbled out into the car's ceiling. Parts of it were still creamy, expensive and soft, like a ship's sail. But it was also full of jagged holes, with snow-encrusted rocks poking through the gaps. Feeling her way through the twisted shapes of the wreck, she found a warm bundle.

'Here you go, First Mate Esme,' she said, unclipping her from her car seat and lifting her down as gently as she could. 'Your big sister pirate queen is free at last, and now this is our ship.'

'Choclit?' said Esme, grinning.

'Yes,' whispered Violet, 'there will be chocolate, whole mountains and factories full of chocolate if you are a brave crew mate and hold on tight. There is going to be chocolate for all, and everything is going to be OK.'

Except how was it going to be OK? They were trapped in a broken, upside-down car in the middle of nowhere, in the worst, coldest winter ever. Their pirate mother was bleeding and not answering questions. Nobody knew they were here. It was Christmas Eve and they were going to miss all the best things about Christmas.

Because even pirates looked forward to getting everything ready for Santa's visit before they went to bed, hanging their stockings up at the end of their hammocks, the excitement of the following morning . . . Oh, the thought of these things only made her feel a million times worse. She didn't even want to think about playing her annual trick on Mouse, where she hid his stocking and he went crazy looking for it.

'Shall I tell you more of that story, Esme?' asked Violet, as she carefully checked her sister for any injuries. 'It's very exciting. Because we need to stay wide awake, don't we?'

'Choclit,' agreed the first mate drowsily.

'Gráinne's husband was called Hugh. She fell in love with him when she rescued him from a shipwreck. He liked hunting deer with a bow and arrow. But one day out in the forest he was killed by Gráinne's enemies.

'This made the pirate queen so sad that she followed her enemies to a remote island, where they had gone on a pilgrimage (which is a journey that is meant to be long and difficult on purpose).

'When she found them they wouldn't apologise so she set fire to all their boats and killed them with her sword. And because all her enemies were now dead, Gráinne took her boat round the coast to their castle, which she conquered and lived in happily for many years.'

First Mate Esme didn't gasp or ooh like Violet's schoolmates in assembly had at this shocking tale. She was very quiet, still and thoughtful as she digested all this new information – which, too late, Violet realised, contained not one crumb of chocolate-related news.

Maybe she could have chosen a story from Gráinne's life with less killing, or one where her enemies went to prison or at least got a parking ticket or something rather than getting murdered. But there weren't too many of those. And it was the truth. It had happened. It said so on the Internet.

She gathered her baby sister close to her, grateful for her warmth. Neither of them was in any kind of state to take on a warring rival pirate clan. But they could still be as tough and fearless as any man or woman to have sailed under the black flag.

'You listen to me, First Mate Esme,' said Violet.

'Choclit,' said First Mate Esme.

'Are you going to be a brave and strong pirate princess for me?'

'Choclit,' repeated Esme softly.

'Because we are going to get through this, I promise. Aren't we?'

First Mate Esme did not reply, but snuggled in closer to her queen. And the two pirates held each other tight, trying to stay warm looking out through the car windows at the white falling all around.

In an explosion of leaves and baa-as, a large sheep bolted out of the copse behind Mouse and ran straight into what remained of the well with a clang of horns on stone. The dinosaur raised his head at this unexpected disruption to his meal.

Bar yanked her horns out of the stonework. 'Baa!' she said, in an am-I-pleased-to-see-you-again kind of a way.

Mouse was pleased to see her too. He wanted to smile at her. But he couldn't, because of the large toy dinosaur about to eat him. And he could also see that, because the sheep was a sheep, and so busy being scared of her own shadow, Bar still hadn't noticed the monster towering over them.

Mouse tried to nod at the dinosaur, as if to say to the

sheep, 'Look up above me. You know, at the ENORMOUS FLIPPING DINOSAUR.'

Bar just nodded back vigorously, saying, 'Baa? Baa!' in a this-is-a-fun-game kind of a way, in between scouring the scrubby ground for anything edible.

Mouse shook his head and waved the sword. He had to make her realise somehow. 'Roar!' he said. 'ROAR!'

'Baa?' said Bar. And she finally looked up.

'ROAR!' roared Trex.

'BAA!' said Bar, because she couldn't say anything else.

Mouse closed his eyes and waited for the inevitable. This was it, for sure, the end of everything.

And he waited some more.

But nothing happened.

And slowly he realised he hadn't counted on two things, which now seemed quite important.

1) Being an ancient sheep from a distant mystical land, Bar had probably never seen a giant plastic toy dinosaur before. It could have been a giant chicken, for all she knew.

2) Equally, being a magically swollen robotic toy, Trex had probably never seen a sheep before. She might have breathed fire, for all he knew.

So the conversation continued more or less like this.

'Roar?' said Trex, a little less loudly.

'Baa!' said Bar, a little more proudly.

Mouse dared to open his eyes. He hadn't been eaten yet, which was good. And as he watched, the most amazing thing happened. Right in front of him, the mutated toy dinosaur was changing shape. His head was no longer the size of a car and he was perhaps now only four or five metres tall. The tail no longer reached the trees. The monster was downsizing before his very eyes.

'Baa!' said Bar in a this-is-very-curious kind of a way, stepping towards the amazing shrinking dinosaur.

'Roar!' gulped Trex in alarm, looking at his claws, then his feet, before straining around to check his tail.

Mouse tucked Wenceslas back in his belt. He was less scared already. The smaller Trex got, the less scary he was. Trex snarled with rage. He didn't seem to like getting smaller. His eyes flashed, and he growled at the sky.

Worried about those jaws again, Mouse took a step back, and Trex stopped shrinking.

In fact he grew a bit bigger again.

Bar didn't look scared though. She looked like she wanted to play, lowering her head and gambolling towards Trex, who began to shrink again as soon as she approached. Mouse was confused. Was the dinosaur going to be small or ginormous? He wished it would make up its mind. But slowly, as the sheep went forward and the dinosaur shrank, and the sheep skipped backwards and the dinosaur swelled up, he began to understand what was happening.

'I get it,' he said, taking a step back. 'It's a game. If I run away from you, or drop my sword, or hide, you get bigger and bigger, don't you?'

Trex swiped a chunk out of the ground with his claws, spraying Bar with mud. Mouse took that as a yes.

'And if I run forward, to play with you . . . ?'

The dinosaur didn't move. Mouse bit his lip, took a deep breath and took a step towards him, once more brandishing Wenceslas. Trex shrank again, until he was only just bigger than a very tall person.

'Gotcha! You can't beat me, Trex – you know I'm the best at games in my year. Especially on PS4.'

The dinosaur looked a bit sad, as if someone had just burst a large balloon that he was holding.

Mouse was beginning to understand the rules of this game. Everything in this world was linked to your thoughts. If you wanted something badly enough, like a horse or a sheep running to your rescue, they appeared. And likewise, if you acted like you weren't scared, nothing bad would happen.

Luckily for Trex, he was still Mouse's favourite other toy, even if he had just tried to eat him. The last thing Mouse wanted to do was make him disappear altogether. So by a careful combination of running forward with Wenceslas, then standing back and looking afraid, Mouse got Trex down to the right size. If he concentrated hard, and didn't look like he was any more or less afraid than this, Mouse reckoned he could keep the dinosaur just as he wanted him. Bar did her best to help by running round and round in ever-decreasing circles.

This right size was not as small as a toy again (which was boring – who would want to go back to that?) and definitely not as scary as a full size T. rex either. It was somewhere in the middle, about the same size as a horse. In fact, exactly the same size as the horse that had just been stolen by a dodgy minstrel.

'Good boy,' said Mouse to Trex, who was looking at him with extreme suspicion. So he tickled the tyrannosaur under the chin, until he closed his eyes and almost seemed to purr. Mouse hadn't thought dinosaurs purred, but he was glad this one did. He hopped on the beast. It was harder than riding a horse, but it was possible to stay on, if you could keep your balance. He stroked Trex on the top of his scaly scalp and they began trotting around the glade on his big chicken legs.

'Faster, Trex!' said Mouse, gripping his neck.

'Hur, hur,' wheezed Trex as he stomped mechanically around, squashing wild flowers and fruit bushes with relish. Round and round the glade they went, Trex's tail sending bluebells and cowslips into the air in bright clouds, Bar chasing after them and bleating with excitement as the pretty colours rained over her fleece. For a moment the sun shone high in the sky, and everyone from dinosaur to boy to sheep was laughing. They were playing, the birds were back on the branches singing and Mouse felt he was having the best time EVER.

And then, as they always do, a cloud passed overhead.

A long grey cloud, that cast them all into a cold and unkind shadow. Once more the cold was at Mouse's back, creeping over him, trying to claim his fingers and his feet. He began to shiver and shake. Trex stopped stomping, his robot eyes frowning in concern.

'Whurh dat?' he asked. (Although Mouse daydreamed during most lessons, he had learned enough to realise that magical robot dinosaurs probably don't speak perfect English.) Bar stopped bleating and huddled next to the pair, for a cruel wind was now whipping through the glade.

Mouse stopped playing and listened. Above the whirr of the robot beneath him, the sheep's teeth chattering and the beating of his own heart, he could hear clanking, hissing and slobbering.

The thing from the Haunted Forest was coming.

It was catching up.

Mouse soon discovered that riding a dinosaur was a bit different to riding a horse. Horses were used to being ridden, and generally went where you directed them, sticking to tracks or paths. Trex just charged, blundering through ferns and brambles, which shredded Mouse's tights. Bar didn't help matters by constantly getting in the way as she zigzagged across the track in excitement.

Neither of them was paying much attention to Mouse's instructions. He was trying very hard to remember where the next cairn was. There was one in the Haunted Forest, in front of the Well of Doom, and after that came . . .

A building of some kind, he was sure of it. Not the castle itself perhaps, although he did keep hoping he might see flags and battlements over the next hill. Mouse kept his eyes peeled for anything that might be a building, but it was difficult when your dinosaur kept swerving all over the place.

Eventually, he could take no more. The hoof prints they had been following faded from view altogether, and even the sheep was exhausted, endlessly nibbling juicy ferns and making can-we-stop-please baas. More worryingly, because he was now so tired, Mouse felt Trex begin to grow into a bigger dinosaur again.

'Right!' he said, tapping him with Wenceslas. 'Let's stop for a break.'

'Shurh!' said the robot dinosaur, promptly throwing him off his back and sending him head over heels into a large spiky fruit bush.

It was the biggest of three bushes, standing together in a cluster. In fact, it was now the *only* bush of the three still remaining. Bar had got there before them and was already reducing the other two to sorry little stumps. Trex applauded, clapping his strange bird claws together. 'Hurh! Hurh!'

But Mouse wasn't worried about those two. Where were Nonky and the minstrel? They couldn't have gone that far. They wouldn't have left him, not Nonky. He never left Nonky anywhere. So that wouldn't be fair.

The air was still. In front of the fruit bushes that his friends were busy eating right to the ground, the grass sloped down towards a rippling brook, which lazily wound its way along below some overhanging branches.

'Hello?' he called out. He wondered if perhaps he could make Nonky appear again just by thinking of her. There was no sign of horse, rider or anything that might be a castle. But above the tinkling water and the relentless munching of the sheep and the dinosaur, Mouse could hear a distant rumbling.

It wasn't the clanking thing, it wasn't the dinosaur and it wasn't a thunderstorm.

It was his stomach.

Before he had felt sleepy, but now he just felt hungry. Starving in fact.

He turned back to look at Bar and Trex stuffing their faces, and had an idea. Searching around in the scrub between his feet, he found a small pile of crumbly-looking fruit – which must have fallen off the bush. Grabbing one before Bar could snaffle it, Mouse took a big bite.

It was a very strange flavour, a mixture of Christmas cake and snow. Who cared? Right now, it was just what he needed.

He almost forgave Bar for eating the bush – who could

blame her? He polished one fruit off in seconds and was about to bite into another, when he heard a noise from further down stream.

Signalling to the others to be quiet, he edged forward to peer through the overhanging branches. He could see, sitting on a patch of riverbank, Sir Dragnet arguing with Nonky. The minstrel looked even more unkempt than before, and now he had a large black eye to add to his collection of stains, tears and scratches.

'Wow!' said Mouse, stepping out of the trees just by them. 'What happened to you? Did you get into a duel?'

Sir Dragnet shook his head and looked away. He looked more sheepish than Bar ever did, which was saying something. Neither of them looked surprised to see him.

'He sang too many songs,' said Nonky. 'We had a little falling-off.'

'Don't you mean a falling-out?'

'No,' said Nonky, stamping her hoofs and making Dragnet jump, 'I mean a falling-*off*.'

'She does and all,' said Dragnet, clutching his lute to his chest. And he began to strum and sing in his high reedy voice.

You can ride a horse to water
But you can't make 'er drink
If you don't do what you oughter
She'll make a right old stink

'Enough, minstrel!' Nonky flicked her tail, and Dragnet nearly dropped the instrument on his toes. The horse eyed the river behind them. 'Or do you want to have a falling-in as well as a falling-off?' She turned back to Mouse. 'So, we meet again. What brings you to this part of town? Something in your eyes tells me it wasn't the view.'

'No. It was . . . you,' was all Mouse said, although he knew that wasn't the full answer.

'I bet you say that to all the pretty horses,' said Nonky.

Mouse felt stupid and embarrassed.

'Well – are you going to climb back on or stand there all day long looking like a wet Wednesday in November?'

'Excuse me, I don't think so, sunshine, thank you very much and kindly,' said Dragnet, standing in front of Nonky. Mouse noticed how, if held in a certain way, a lute easily became a threatening weapon. 'You may not respect my art, but the law of the land requires you respect my terms. I demand payment for my dragon song.'

Mouse smiled. The one good thing about riding a dinosaur for hours in eighteen different directions through brambles is that it gave you plenty of time to think. 'Did you say you would accept dragon treasure?'

'Coins, bars of gold, silver nuggets, precious stones, dragon treasure and—'

'How about an actual dragon?'

Dragnet smirked. 'Very droll, sunshine. But we don't accept jests. Hard currency only, I'm afraid.' He gave a nasty sneer and stuck out his hand. 'As long as you are in my debt, I get to ride the horse, and you get to walk.'

'But you would you accept a dragon?'

Dragnet's eyes narrowed. 'Ye-es, my little lordling. But it must be a dragon – a whole dragon. Not a dragon's tooth, or a branch of dragonroot, or a dragon in an illuminated manuscript.'

'What's an illuminated manuscript?' said Mouse, frowning.

'Monks, pictures, takes ages, looks lovely in a museum,' snapped Dragnet. 'You get my point.'

'A real dragon,' promised Mouse, sticking out his hand again.

'Yes, a *real* dragon,' said the minstrel mockingly. He took Mouse's hand like it was a large slug and gave it one brief limp shake. Nonky watched on with an expressionless stare. If she knew what Mouse was up to, her eyes gave nothing away.

Mouse put two fingers in his mouth and whistled.

At his call, the large robot dinosaur rose majestically from behind the trees and the Christmas-cake fruit bush, where he had been having the shortest of naps.

'Th-that's not a dragon,' stammered the minstrel, recoiling from the monster's colossal shadow. In reply, Trex bent down, opened his jaws and roared so loudly that Sir Dragnet's floppy jester's hat billowed out like a windsock and the man nearly floated up into the sky.

'OK, he's a dragon, I believe you, just make him stop,' he said, cowering. Trex was beginning to grow, sniffing the waves of fear washing out from the minstrel.

'Play nicely, Trex,' Mouse said, tapping the robot monster on his flank with Wenceslas. Trex stopped growing.

'Helorgh,' he said to the minstrel, who had gone the same colour as the winter sky. Trex held out a large robot reptile claw for him to shake.

'Very charmed, I'm sure,' said Sir Dragnet, scowling at them both. He tried to climb on to the dinosaur's back, and immediately slid down the other side, landing flat on his face in a muddy puddle. Wiping the mud off, he tried the other way, only this time he slipped down the dinosaur's tail. He tried once more, but his lute and strap got tangled around Trex's leg, and after untangling lute from leg, finally he clambered on.

'Aha!' he said, and a gust of wind blew his hat off into the bog.

Everyone was laughing at him, including Bar, who had finally finished all the fruit and was looking for some after-dinner entertainment. Mouse was doubled up, which made the handle of his sword press hard into his guts. Bar's 'baa-baa' sounded suspiciously like 'haa-haa', even Nonky was whinnying with excitement and Trex was gurgling, 'Yurgh! Yurgh!' (Mouse flushed with pleasure. Maybe he was only little, but he had made a dinosaur laugh, and who else in Year 6 could say that?)

'If you don't stop laughing, I shall . . . I shall . . . sing a song!' blustered Dragnet, who had gone very red in the face.

This only made Mouse laugh more. At last he really was beginning to properly, actually enjoy this story he was in, in this funny new world with its games, strange-tasting fruit and incompatible animals.

Another wind blew in. Dragnet kept his hat firmly

pressed to his head this time, the bells tinkling in the breeze. This wind was colder, and as it rushed past them, the day grew a little darker. With the wind came not only the night, and the frost at Mouse's back, but a sound. The hissing, clanking and slobbering that kept them moving ever on in search of the castle.

'I'm afraid that clanking noise means only one thing,' said Nonky.

'You don't need to keep telling me,' said Mouse. 'I'm not deaf, only small.' He got back on top of Nonky. 'I know. We need to find the castle before that thing does. And I'm beginning to see how.'

'Congratulations,' said Nonky. 'I'll update your Wikipedia entry as soon as I can get some signal, out here in the Middle Ages. But first, maybe you'd like to tell me where to go next.'

Only a short while ago Mouse would have stammered and stumbled. But now he had not only tamed a dragon, but also fooled a wily minstrel. Perhaps it was the Christmas-cake fruit, but his head was buzzing, his blood was pumping and he was so cold he almost felt hot.

'I don't know exactly,' he said, 'but I do know we're looking for cairns that lead to the castle, and I think the next one is by a building.'

Nonky stared at him. 'And?'

'And I think it's . . . that way,' he said, pointing into the distance where the brook disappeared under a plain of marshy reeds.

'*I think it's that way?*' repeated Nonky slowly. 'Let me give you some career advice, little knight. Fifteen years from now, when they advertise that job in air-traffic control, don't apply. Deal?'

Mouse no longer cared how sarcastic his horse was, or how ripped his tights were. He was full of Christmas-cake fruit – although not as full as a certain sheep – and nothing was going to stop him. 'Deal!' he declared, beaming.

With that, Nonky set off through the reeds of the valley, her sleek black hindquarters swaying from side to side, as the dinosaur, minstrel and sheep hurried after. Not one of them turned around to see what was behind them.

But there was something there.

It stopped by the remains of the fruit bush. It bent down and picked up one of the fruits Mouse had taken a bite from. It sniffed the fruit all over, inhaling the scent of its prey.

And it laughed. It wasn't a nice laugh. Not a nice laugh at all.

Captain Violet O'Belty was beginning to realise that if she kept promising her one crew member chocolate, eventually she was going to have to produce some. Chocolate was coming, she said again and again, until it sounded like she was trying to persuade herself more than Esme.

'Try and sit tight, first mate. Don't worry – chocolate is coming.'

Ideally in an ambulance or a fire engine, she thought but didn't say.

'Choclit!' said Esme, more insistent than before. She seemed convinced that chocolate had to be on board somewhere.

Violet had already searched the entire wreck twice. But their ship's stores had only offered up a tin containing half of a smashed Christmas cake (who knew where the other half had got to). She knew well that you had to preserve rations when stranded at sea, so she stuffed her pockets with the remains, determined not to eat them all at once.

But First Mate Esme was not so easily convinced.

'Christmas cake, first mate?' Violet said, offering her a messy handful of crumbs and raisins.

'Choclit.'

'How about just the icing? Look, it's the one we made together last week. Remember?'

'CHOCLIT!'

Esme was going to start crying if Violet didn't do something soon. She didn't want her to start crying, for lots of reasons. Partly because the car was so small, partly because Esme's crying was so ear shattering and mainly . . . because she really didn't want her to cry.

Violet looked around in the darkness at the misshapen wreck. There were no two ways about it. They were trapped.

'How about my story, first mate? Would you like to hear more about the pirate queen?'

'Choclit,' mumbled Esme.

'I'll take that as a yes. Well, once some enemy soldiers trapped Gráinne in her castle on an island. They didn't let her bring in any food or drink, and doing that is called a siege. So the pirate queen commanded her men to melt

118

down the lead roof of the castle into musket bullets. They shot at the soldiers, who had to retreat. But the siege continued. So Gráinne sent one of her men through a secret tunnel to the mainland, where he lit a bonfire beacon to call for reinforcements.'

Esme was beginning to wriggle. Violet tried to keep going.

'You see, Gráinne won lots of battles because she did not panic under pressure but thought things through, unlike her enemies. Which is what we're doing, isn't it?'

But her little sister wasn't having any of it, slipping free of her grasp to play in the debris. It was almost like she was looking for something.

Oh well. Violet shrugged. What would Gráinne do in this situation? She began to make a list of their immediate problems, starting with the snow and the cold outside. Next was whatever injuries were keeping her mother asleep and making her bleed. Not to mention a broken car that couldn't go anywhere, and nobody knowing where they were. And feeling hungry and tired.

'Choclit,' added Esme, who appeared to have found her toothbrush again, gently banging the stick of plastic against the rubber seal of the window, whose other side was coated with frost. She made horse noises as the toothbrush trotted along the black cliff-top of the window seal.

Whoops, horsey fell off! Hooray, horsey climbed back on again.

Next the toothbrush seemed to become a boat, cruising and sliding along the rubber line. Or was it a spaceship or, turned vertical on its tip, a lady in a furry hat?

Violet sighed. It was easy to make things up and tell stories, about pirates or horses or anything in the world. It was much less easy, she was discovering, to unmake them when they happened to you in real life.

Esme was suddenly aware of her older sister studying her and, pouting, she hid the brush away under the folds of her jacket. 'Choclit,' she said defensively.

No, chocolate was not the answer. What they needed was proper help from the outside. More than anything else, Violet wanted to be rescued. She racked her brains. Could anything Gráinne had done help them?

She had melted shot. Ordered beacons to be lit.

Violet O'Belty's heart rose and then sank. It was cold and wet, and there was nothing they could make a fire with. No one knew precisely where they were, but Granny and Gramps must be worried by now. They would be searching for them, surely?

As if Esme could sense her sister's worry, she wriggled and kicked, letting out a violent shriek. 'CHOCLIT!'

'Don't worry, First Mate Esme,' said Captain Violet. 'I'm looking for some. So keep on doing that with your toothbrush. Making stuff up. It's nice, isn't it?'

'Choclit!' shouted Esme again, and flung the toothbrush to the floor in rage.

Perhaps Violet could at least turn the engine on and keep them warm.

'Yes,' she said, squeezing through the twisted seat gap to the front. 'There will be chocolate, I promise.'

She was nearly able to reach the key, dangling out of the socket.

'CHOCLIT! CHOCLIT!' screamed Esme, tears starting to slide down her cheeks.

'Just wait, Esme,' snapped Violet. 'I'll give you some more rations in a minute.'

Captain Violet O'Belty focused and tried to reach for the key. But her mother was in the way. Violet couldn't move her or climb over her. She was too heavy, and she really didn't want to risk hurting her more than she was already.

Esme began to really wail. The word *choclit* mingled with wet tears and sniffing. Her cries echoed inside the car, rising above the sound of her mother's breathing, drifting out of the broken windows, up and away into the cold night air. They rose up in the dark towards the stars, above the pointed treetops and out across the whole frozen valley, searching for anyone who would hear.

'I bet Gráinne O'Malley never had to put up with this,' sighed Violet. But she withdrew her hand from the gap between the seats and crawled back to her sister. 'Come on, First Mate Esme,' she said, and tried to give her a cuddle.

But First Mate Esme was not in a cuddling mood. More than proving her pirate skills, she gave the front passenger seat a hefty kick. 'Choclit!' she insisted.

Captain Violet felt like she should put the first mate in the hold, or whatever you did with pirates who misbehaved. 'Come on, Esme, I've told you there's no chocolate. What do you want me to do?'

'No, choclit!' said Esme louder, kicking again with her foot.

'And stop kicking! You might hit Mum, and that's the last thing she needs.'

Her first mate looked worried for a nanosecond, before kicking again, twice as hard. Except she wasn't kicking, was she, realised Captain O'Belty. She was pointing, with her feet, at something lying on the jumbled ceiling (now floor) of the car. At first, O'Belty thought she meant her book, which was splayed open, all creased and torn. Then she looked closer, and saw her book was covering a shadowy bar, which stuck out from between the rumpled pages.

'You mean this?' said Violet, pointing.

Esme nodded vigorously. 'Choclit,' she said, and clasped her hands together, almost as if in prayer.

Her captain sank to her knees, crawling around in the sea of upended bags and junk, along the ripped roof of the car, until she reached the book and grabbed the bar. As she did, she closed her eyes in relief. Violet O'Belty had nearly forgotten the second testament of her heroine.

Gráinne O'Malley always trusted her crew. She thought loyalty more important than anything else.

The captain brandished the bar in her first mate's face, crying with joy, 'Look, Esme, look! It must have fallen out of his pocket when he fell out of the car!'

Esme licked her lips in anticipation. 'Choclit! Choclit!' she cried with joy, clapping her hands together. But her face fell, as Violet didn't unwrap the bar, but began tapping on it. A hard look of disappointment crept into the first mate's eyes as the bar began to glow.

Violet didn't care. Sometimes you didn't need to make the answers up. Sometimes they were staring you right in the face all along. True, Esme hadn't actually found any chocolate. She had found something a thousand times better.

Mouse's mobile phone.

As they splashed softly through the marshy valley, one single question burned and bubbled in Mouse's head. It was not a good question. And he guessed the answer would be even worse.

He tried to bite his tongue as they rode out of the boggy plain and on to a track that was still muddy but less spongy. He tried really hard to think of something else as they followed this track through a narrow chasm, a small gap in the mountain walls overhung by a thorny briar. He ordered himself to focus on looking for the next cairn, scanning the horizon for anything that might be a building.

But he just couldn't help it. He had to know what was following them.

Nonky jerked to a halt, feeling him fidget and start to

twist around. 'Don't even think about it, buster,' she said.

'I'm not doing anything,' Mouse lied, trying to look behind without moving his hips at all, which was difficult.

'Once you've done it, you can't undo it,' warned the horse.

'What does it matter? I'm not doing anything,' said Mouse.

'Sure. If you don't trust me, go right ahead. Be my guest, compadre. Turn around. Stand on my back and do the hokey-cokey if you really want. But don't say I didn't warn you.'

'How bad can it be?' said Mouse, and spun one-hundred and eighty degrees in his saddle, so he was looking at Sir Dragnet, Trex and Bar. If he was making this story up, if he was somehow imagining the characters and the world, what was the worst thing he could think of?

Surely he couldn't really imagine anything so truly powerful and dangerous that he couldn't defeat it? Trex was a T. rex for goodness sake, and he was eating out of his hand.

What harm was there in looking back when you were telling a story?

'I should heed your noble steed if were you, sunshine,' said Dragnet, and this time there was no trace of a wink or a smile on his face. 'You may not fancy what you clap your peepers on, and no mistake.'

'Don't you want to see what's following us, Sir Dragnet?'

'He's not following us, my boy. That's the rub. He's following you.'

Mouse's cheeks flushed with anger. 'If he's only following me, why are you all so scared of him? What's it got to do with any of you anyway? I'm the knight. I'm the one looking for the castle, aren't I? I'm the one he wants to . . . you know.'

He couldn't say that word. He didn't even want to think about that word. It was too . . . stressful. So, defiantly, he stared past them. Bar sadly shook her head. 'Urgh-orgh,' whispered Trex, slowly beginning to swell. Nonky gave a long, low sigh.

Mouse ignored them all and concentrated hard on the opening in the mountain walls behind them, where the path disappeared back into shadow. He could still hear the hissing and slobbering, but there was nothing to see. 'I knew it,' he said. 'You're just making it all up to scare me. It's another game, like the one with Trex. And I'm really good at games. Why don't you take a look to see for yourself? There's nothing there.'

Dragnet stubbornly glowered at him from the back of

the dinosaur, refusing to turn even an inch. Mouse was about to make another cutting remark, when something began to emerge from the mist, pushing aside the thorny briar. It was hard to see at first as it dragged its heavy feet into view.

An armoured boot, splashing into the mud, followed by another.

The boots weren't so much taking steps, more heaving themselves over the ground, as if their burden was too heavy to lift. Mouse felt a tingle of recognition as he saw them, which turned into a jolt as their owner staggered into the half-light.

'That's impossible,' he said.

It couldn't be. Except there it was, in front of his very eyes. Huge and horribly hunched at the same time, one chain-mail arm dangling so low that its knuckled gauntlet scraped along the ground. The breastplate was scratched and filthy, the plume on the helmet hanging limp, surrounded by a cloud of flies. But there was no mistaking the colour, muddied and tarnished as it was, that ran from the tip of his helm to the ends of his boots.

Pink.

It was the Pink Knight from his iPad game.

Mouse stared at the Pink Knight, and the Pink Knight stared right back. The knight had been on his side in Junior Joust, but something told him that game was definitely over.

At the same time he spotted a small hedgehog trundle out from under the briar, sniffing the air, its bright little eyes like blackcurrants. Seeing the strange knight, the creature squeaked with fear and rolled up into a spiky ball.

Mouse tensed, his shoulders and neck tight, his hand on Wenceslas at his side. But the knight didn't pull his own rusted sword out of its scabbard in response. Nor did he remove the axe from the strap over his back. He didn't say a word. Instead, with his chain-mailed fingers, he fiddled with hooks on his huge helmet, and the pair of hinged cheek-pieces covering his jaw swung open, dangling to the side.

The hedgehog flinched at the clanging metal noise but stayed curled up where it was.

So it did not see what Mouse saw. Beneath the knight's helmet hung a long black beard. A very dense, tangled mass of hair. It quite covered his mouth and chin and was the strangest and blackest beard Mouse thought he had ever seen, as if it sucked out all colour from the day. Yet there was something stranger still. As he watched, the beard seemed to grow. The wedge of thick curls grew and unfurled down to the ground.

And Mouse realised, with a lurch, that it wasn't a beard at all.

It was just blackness – oily tendrils of smoke that curled out of the Pink Knight's jaw. It spilled down to his feet, as if his neck was a spurting fountain of ink, and began to drift along the ground towards the boy. As it spilled towards him, the reeds it touched wilted and shrivelled. The grass withered. The light from the sun itself seemed to vanish from the ground where the beard spread.

The hedgehog unrolled with a violent squeak of alarm and tried to scurry back towards the briars. Mouse watched in horror as it trotted straight into the creeping fumes. The smoke seemed to pass harmlessly through the animal at first. But when the cloud had moved on, there remained only a shrivelled sack of spikes and skin lying flat on the ground, as if the beard had sucked it clean of all living matter.

Mouse began to feel unwell. His stomach roiled with pulpy bolts of nausea. Sweat slicked down his neck and forehead, stinging his eyes.

'Nonky,' he said, his teeth chattering. 'Can we go, please? Hurry.'

The horse didn't seem in any great rush though. 'Excuse me for a moment while I flick back through my diary . . . Oh yes. I seem to have had a conversation with you EXACTLY TWO MINUTES AGO where I recall telling you not, under any circumstances, to turn around. And now look what you've done.'

The Pink Knight bent over, like he was retching something up. More blackness spewed out. It was in the air, clouding towards them, like a swarm of locusts. It scratched out the trees and the sky. It was . . . nothing. Everything the beard touched turned to oblivion.

'I know you did, Nonky, I'm sorry . . . but please!' He was only just able to wrench himself away from the knight and the blackness pouring out of him. The second he was facing away, the horse muttered, 'As you command, little knight,' and they were all off, scrambling away up the track, hoping upon hope that the next cairn was not far away.

But the Pink Knight did not follow them.

He stood there, in his bubble gum-coloured armour, swaying silently. He did not replace his jaw-piece, or speak, or give off any sound other than the creaking of his metal joints and the wind whistling through the grille of his helmet. He was hungry and he needed to feed.

Like all experienced hunters, he knew that the waiting and watching was the most important part. So he did nothing at first. He stood and waited, not moving or speaking, until the darkness of the night fell around him, lit only by the icy glare of the moon in the sky. The valley was still, apart from the occasional flap of a bird on a branch, a rustle in the grass.

Until, finally, the time for waiting was over.

Before him, the cloud of his poisonous beard still seeped over the rocks, rushes, flowers and creatures it had touched. Every stone underneath its veil was cracked, every branch was blackened, every petal rotten, every living thing a parched husk. But as the day vanished, and the moonlight fell, the black beard-cloud began to stir again.

It fizzed and trembled, licking some of the withered objects into a new being.

They were only simple things, bits of the earth – a rock, a bush and a log. The blackness burst into flames over their lifeless shapes, and out of the fire arose something new and awful.

Eyes welled up in the surface of the rock, as red as blood. The bush sprouted thorny jointed legs like a spider. Inside the hollow opening of the log, dripping fangs appeared as if in a mouth. These things of nature had seen so much. They had been walked upon, run upon, rained upon, weathered, beaten and wind-dashed. They had died and been reborn. Before they were a rock or a log or a bush, they had been something else. A mountain, a tree, a seed caught on the wind.

But now they were only things of death.

With bent legs, slavering jaws and flicking tails, they were the Pink Knight's demon hounds. Hard beasts made of stone, wood and thorn. They frisked about his legs, whining and skittish, straining for the scent. The knight bent down and slowly unfolded his heavy gauntlet. In his palm, soft and gentle against the grainy mail, lay the remains of Mouse's Christmas-cake fruit. Greedily the hounds of earth sniffed, snorting up the scent.

They sat on their haunches and howled to the moon. The knight reached across his back and drew from a leather holder a thin and twisted pipe, about the length of his arm. The Pink Knight stuck the pipe into the shadows of his maw, and blew.

The sound was loud and harsh. It broke the calm of the night sky, sending rooks circling into the air with terror. His hounds went berserk, barking and biting each other's tails. The call of the knight's horn rang out over the valleys and mounds and tracks and moats of this land, shaking leaves from the trees and sending ripples through ponds.

With a roar, the hounds set off at a gallop, haring over the earth. They ran so fast, they scarcely touched the ground. Behind them, the Pink Knight drove his pack forward. Reaching under his helmet, he plucked free a single black hair. With one vile gust of his breath, he transformed this into a whip, which he used to spur them on ever faster.

Further away, on a distant hillside, a horse in shining armour paused. The boy on her back sat and listened. 'What's that sound?' he said.

'A horn,' said Nonky. And she began to really run.

The horn.

'Why didn't I think of that before, First Mate Esme? It's what Dad would have done, isn't it? I mean, our pirate father.'

She pressed down on the steering-wheel panel again with all her weight, and the ship's foghorn sounded another blast across the lonely sea while the first mate looked on.

'Choclit,' she muttered to herself, somewhat bitterly.

'I know,' said her captain with effort, as she pressed once more. 'Not only was it not chocolate, but it didn't even work.' She had been very pleased with herself at remembering Mouse's passcode – which of course she knew; she was his sister – only to find that his phone had no signal. No bars at all, just those two awful words: 'No Service'. Violet had held it out of the window, shaken it, turned it upside down – nothing.

There was one tantalising moment as she half pushed her hand out of the car window with the phone, like a worm out of a hole, when there was a glimmer of a bar and the screen flashed hopefully. But after a few seconds it disappeared, and no matter what angle Violet got herself or the phone into again, the bar stubbornly refused to return.

So she turned the handset off, to save battery power. It could always be used as a torch instead. No doubt her phone or Mum's were also somewhere in this tip. Or perhaps they had been thrown out through the windscreen when they crashed. She wasn't going to start looking for them now, not at night, as the temperature fell, and fell.

'Someone is bound to hear the horn, aren't they, first mate?'

'Beep-beep!' Esme agreed, stamping her feet.

It was funny. Despite the phone not working, despite there being no sign of anyone coming or even having heard the horn, Violet felt better. Like Gráinne, she was taking action in a crisis. She was trying all the options and getting a message out.

And she knew it wasn't just Gráinne inspiring her.

Dad would not have approved of the phone option. He was always telling them off for having their faces stuck to a screen. 'What's wrong with the real world?' he used to say, flinging the door open and chasing them outside. Dad had built a tree house in the garden, showing them how to choose a good tree with two sturdy branches forming a V for your main support. He showed Violet how to use a drill and a lathe and how to seal the wood to protect it. They all built it together. Dad would rather play football than watch TV, preferred to go looking for frogs in their pond than shopping, and if he could give you a homemade present rather than one 'made in some blooming factory' he would. So it was interesting that he had left them all for someone he had met online.

'One more go,' said the captain. 'Block your ears, first mate!'

She pressed down on the horn hard again, reaching over her mum as carefully as she could. The sound wallowed out of the crumpled bonnet, bouncing off the pine trees and shattered stone wall, before being swallowed up by the blankets of snow.

The phone not working had been the worst thing, Violet had to admit. To cheer herself up, she had managed to turn the engine on and run the heating for a bit, but she grew worried about how much fuel was left in the tank, so turned it off again.

'Why doesn't it sound louder, Esme? Can you tell me that?'

'BEEP-BEEP!' Esme bellowed obligingly.

'No, first mate, I meant – oh, never mind.'

Surely someone would hear though. They couldn't be that far from everywhere. Granny and Gramps would have called the police, the ambulance, even the fire brigade. She knew they would. Maybe even the army. Gramps was a doctor after all; he knew all the right people and what to do.

Surely if she kept pressing, the sound would wake someone up.

Surely at least it would wake up Mum, thought Violet, digging her elbows into her mother's chest, but trying really hard not to. The problem was, everything was getting harder to do. Violet's breaths were starting to come in icy rasps down her throat. Her muscles felt weak, and pushing a horn which was normally as easy as squashing a cushion now felt more like pressing down on a great bellows.

'Come *on*,' she said in a tight voice. 'Someone. Mum. Someone, please.'

'My mummy,' said Esme in an even smaller voice from the bottom of the wreck.

'I know, Esme, I know. We all want Mum. She'll be awake soon. I promise.'

But despite her brave and inspiring words to her crew, Captain Violet O'Belty felt, indeed knew, that time was running out.

Not just time, but fuel and Christmas cake.

Some inner instinct was telling her that the most important thing was to stay warm — for all of them to stay warm. Her mother was ashen. And her body temperature — as far as Violet could tell — was dropping.

'But we are going to stay nice and snug together, aren't we, first mate?' she said to her sister, hugging her even tighter. Her sister was beginning to feel cold too. Really cold. As was she. For the first time, the captain even found herself doubting Gráinne O'Malley.

'I know she was the best pirate queen in the world ever, first mate,' said Violet, her teeth chattering. 'But I am never again dressing up as her to go on a long journey in cold weather.'

At least, not when the only pirate clothing option available was her dad's old dressing gown.

Sitting bolt upright, she remembered full well, in fact, that Gráinne herself would not have made such a mistake. Why on earth hadn't she thought of this before, instead of fiddling with a mobile phone —

Pirates didn't just wear skull-and-crossbones hats and eyepatches in the olden days — the sea was very cold and so they would also wear sheepskin and furs. Often they stole these rather than buying them.

In the boot were bags containing not sheepskin or furs, but fleece hoodies and Gore-Tex anoraks. The captain twisted round and stretched her hand out into this hold, and with great difficulty – due to the angle at which the ship had grounded – tried to reach for the chest containing these warming garments.

The zip of her favourite camouflage bag – not the actual bag, just the zip sewn into a flopping flap of fabric – was within her grasp. The other bags and cases had slid too far into the corner. She tried to grip the tiny nub of metal with her freezing fingers, and pull, but the bag was just too heavy to lift that way.

Of course.

Violet had packed more books than she needed. Why did she always do that? And what kind of self-respecting pirate queen took books on a mission anyway? It was Christmas; they would spend most of the time eating and watching telly. But you never knew when you would want to escape from everyone and drift off to a different world. Maybe next time she might pack those worlds electronically.

If there was a next time . . .

No. She mustn't think like that. She must *never* think like that. There would always be a next time. An ambulance, the police, a farmer, a space satellite – someone or something was going to discover and rescue them soon, just like in the movies.

'Everything is going to be all right,' she told herself. 'Isn't it, Esme? Everything is going to be all right.'

The bag of winter coats and books slipped from her fingers and further out of sight.

Violet bit her lip and tried again.

Deep breaths, Gráinne told herself.

Violet paused, her hand dangling over the elusive zip. For a moment there, she realised, she had thought she *was* Gráinne O'Malley. Not remembering her deeds from a school project, or pretending to be her, she had felt as if she *was* her. As if her mind had slipped out of place. Suddenly she remembered a dream she had had the other night about walking along a window ledge, and it felt *real*. She wondered if the breakfast she had eaten earlier – which felt like a very long time ago – was real or a dream?

What was happening?

She paused for breath, flicking damp hair back from her forehead, and reached for the bag again. With a final tug it came loose, upsetting Mum's bin liner of presents all over the boot. That didn't matter. They all looked battered and torn anyway.

Once upon a time, Violet thought, the sight of such lovely

Christmas presents ruined so completely would have reduced her to tears. Right this second though, she couldn't care less. She had something much better – coats, jumpers, hats, gloves and scarves. They were old, tatty and in no way could any of them be described as matching.

Yet to the pirate queen at this moment, they were such treasures as she never could have dreamed of, and she laid them like cloths of silk over her sleeping mother, wrapped them around the first mate like the rarest fur and pulled a big sweatshirt over her head as if it was the most delicate and finest lambswool.

They had not escaped or found help. She had a feeling that they were not going to wake up to bulging stockings from Father Christmas left on the bonnet. But, by every pirate charm and talisman in this world, there was a chance they might just get warm enough to grab some sleep.

Further up the valley, following only Mouse's gut instinct for directions, the horse and her rider flew like the wind.

Or at least they tried to. No matter how much Nonky strained and sweated, it felt to Mouse like they were wading through treacle. Still, they all struggled on: him on a warrior horse, followed by a minstrel clinging to a dinosaur and a waddling sheep with curly horns. It might have been funny.

But it wasn't.

Because as he and his friends gasped for breath, branches springing back into their faces, boulders grazing Nonky's shins, the night air scalding their throats, the only feeling they knew was fear. They had left the Haunted

Forest far behind (though not its creature), passed the Well of Doom, waded through a marsh and squeezed through a thorny chasm.

They found themselves up a hill lined with trees that cast stark shadows like scarecrows, and Mouse tried not to think about what was hiding in the gaps between.

Things were chasing them, things they couldn't see but could hear. He couldn't tell how many things there were, but they seemed to be coming at them from all sides. Their howls echoed up to the moon, which glared at them from behind smoky wisps of cloud. It wasn't just howls Mouse could hear, but growls, grunts and snaps. Every now and then, there was a crack of a whip.

He wanted to ask Nonky what was going on, who was chasing them, but the horse seemed so focused on where she was going, and how fast she was moving, that he didn't dare. Instead he clung on, burying his face in her warm mane and trying not to cry.

At the top of the hill he could see a stark line of jagged silhouettes. More trees perhaps? As the horse got closer and closer, her body seeming to sketch to cover the distance, he could see they were not trees, but stones.

Rows and rows of stones, in fact. Some were taller than others, some were straight and some were crooked.

And behind them loomed a dark block, shrouded by swirls of mist.

A tower! Could it be what they were looking for? He peered into the gloom . . . No. Not a castle, just a tower.

Mouse dared to turn and look behind him. What more harm could it do? He had looked once already. It couldn't be anything worse than what he had seen before, the Pink Knight with the toxic black beard.

Except it was.

There were creatures chasing them –

With bloody eyes and jutting fangs –

Slathering as they loped towards them across the slope.

'Faster, Nonky,' he gasped, as if he was doing the galloping and not her. 'Faster!'

The sheep was bleating for her life, for the first time not even pausing to eat a single blade of grass, and now Trex looked scared too. He should have been growing big from everyone else's fear, but that was impossible when he had the fear as well.

Mouse could smell rancid breath, hear a thunderous gallop, sense razor teeth only an inch from their quarry, chomping and frothing –

He closed his eyes.

'Duck!' said the horse.

Mouse opened his eyes just in time to see a low beam underneath a wooden roof, dripping with wet. He crouched low and they clattered through the gateway, the grass giving way to paving under Nonky's hoofs. They were right under the tower, surrounded by rows of stones. Nonky's breathing was long and strained, sucking air right into the bottom of her lungs. Trex, Bar and Sir Dragnet piled in after them, collapsing on the ground in a heap of lute, tail and horns.

Mouse tumbled off Nonky, trying to reach for Wenceslas –

But the hounds of earth did not come through the wooden archway, even though the gate stood wide open. Instead they pawed at the railings that ran around the rows of stones with their claws, whining, their demonic eyes rolling in their misshapen skulls. Below them, the Pink Knight wheezed his way up the hill. When he lumbered into view he cracked his whip of Mouse's hair against his armoured thigh with a groan of disappointment and began striding around the fence, examining it.

'What is it, Nonky?' whispered Mouse, peering wide-eyed over the horse's pommel at the monsters in the moonlight beyond. 'Why can't they come in?'

'Why do you think? When did you last take a shower,

kiddo? They'd be overpowered by the fumes, for starters.'

'Seriously.'

'Seriously? I don't do seriously – doctor's orders. But maybe it's something to do with the fact that those who would drag you into the grave have no power if you are actually already there.'

'You mean—'

He stopped, and looked around him. Sir Dragnet had gone very pale and was resting with a hand on the nearest stone, running his fingers over the ridges and markings carved into it. Bar sniffed the air, and Trex sat in a heap on the ground, looking very small for a dinosaur indeed.

There was something strange about this place. It looked from the outside just like rows of stones with tufts of grass at their base. He remembered seeing them somewhere before. Had he gone for a walk past one with someone once? Was this the next landmark? Trying to ignore the growls and yelps just metres away, he sheathed Wenceslas and began to inspect the stones.

They weren't all the same shape. There were square ones, and curved ones. They were straight, slanted or square, like stone tables. Some had sculptures on top, hooded angels with pointed wings, which looked as if they could swoop down at any moment.

'Don't go far,' said Nonky.

Mouse wasn't listening. He found himself wandering further and further among the rows of stones that crowned the hillside. In places they had crumbled near away to nothing, or were pulled to the side by knots of ivy. The grass felt soft underfoot, and there was a chill to the air.

As he walked around, he saw that the tower was attached to a building, which was shut and dark. A building! He was looking for one of those, even if it was all locked up. The only light came from the moon as it emerged from behind the clouds, shining down against the high windows.

All of a sudden, Mouse found himself far away from his friends.

He remembered what Nonky had said, and tried to go back. He should look for the cairn. But the standing stones were like a maze, and he couldn't remember where he had last seen his companions.

Everywhere he looked, he saw names. They all seemed so similar.

There were dates too, from times long ago. He went this way, and that way –

All he could see were faces and hands, arms, reaching out for him –

They were statues made of marble and stone. The heads

of old men with whiskery side chops, next to figures of young children, his age. Knights in armour, curled up with swords, their wives asleep on marble beds beside them or wiping away tears at their feet. Tall crosses with Celtic rings that listed to one side, and heavy ribbed urns, eaten away by moss and the wind. There were garlands and swags, engraved poppies and sculpted oak leaves, birds taking flight or ships in full sail, but all of it so cold, white and still.

They couldn't move.

Except in his mind. And without meaning to at all, Mouse remembered that he was very good at making things up. Which was when the statues started to whistle.

It was the kind of steady, low whistle that someone might make while resting against the wall on a street corner, waiting for someone. Up and down the whistle went from the gravestones – because he now realised that was what they were. This was where the next cairn was. It had to be. The tower was part of the church; that was the building he had been looking for. The Church of No Electricity. Why did he know to call it that? Then he remembered that there was also a pile of rocks by the front gate – if only he was brave enough to go out there and look for it.

They were a step nearer to the castle, but he wished to be anywhere but here.

Steady and slow went the whistle, a sad tune. The old men, their carved eyes bulging in their face as they whistled; a young girl, frozen in play for ever, her lips pursed; the knight sitting upright with his sword . . .

The tune surrounded him. He backed away, putting his hands out.

'No!' he said. 'I don't want to, I'm not—'

Because he knew that was why they were whistling. The hounds had driven him here, and they didn't need to come in. The dead were already waiting for him.

Mouse took another step back, then another –

And fell into a hole.

Mouse picked himself up. He was in some kind of ditch – a deep one. If he looked up, he could see the moonlight creeping through the tufts of grass around the edge. The walls were roughly dug, and the ground was lumpy. There were fragments of stone, or wood, or worse, beneath his feet.

For about the first time in this story of his, he knew exactly where he was. And he didn't like it.

If there was one thing he knew about good stories, it was that the hero doesn't get buried in the middle of them. So why was he in a grave? At least he was alone in here, he thought with a shudder, although he didn't investigate too closely. Mouse stood on his toes and stretched his arms, straining for the moon. If only he was bigger, he might have been able to jump or climb out.

If only he was bigger. Mouse hung his head in despair.

He wasn't bigger. He wasn't big enough to climb out of a stupid grave. He wasn't big enough to find the castle. And the people he was finding the castle for – not only had he forgotten their names, but now he was never going to see them again.

Nonky stuck her head into the hole, blocking out the moonlight. 'I thought I might find you in here,' she sighed. 'I don't know. Kids these days, always jumping ahead to see what happens at the end.'

If she was trying to make a joke, Mouse didn't see the funny side. 'Nonky, I think I've fallen into a grave by mistake.'

'Congratulations! Collect two hundred pounds and Do Not Pass Go.'

'It's not funny! I don't like it in here. In fact, I really hate graves,' Mouse said. 'They're dark and old and smell weird.'

'You mean as opposed to all those millions of people who really love graves?' said the horse.

Mouse's bottom lip wobbled.

'None of that, little knight,' said Nonky. 'Come, come. Not yet.' She turned and neighed behind her. 'Dragnet!

Get your useless minstrel behind over here and help our hero out of his latest hole.'

Before Mouse knew what was happening, Sir Dragnet had jumped into the grave with him, and was grabbing him around the waist, hoisting him up. Trex's spiny tail was dangling over the edge, and Mouse grabbed it, pulling himself on to the damp grass. Bar trotted over, nuzzling him back into warmth, bleating in an it's-really-lucky-it-wasn't-me-who-fell-down-that-hole-because-that-would-have-been-a-whole-other-story kind of a way.

Mouse grabbed the tufts of the sheep's wool gratefully, holding her close to him. Then he slumped down to the ground, leaning against one of the big gravestones shaped like an altar. It was surprisingly comfortable, and didn't appear to be whistling.

'Can we get out of here now, please?' he said, shivering.

'Sorry, kid,' said Nonky. 'Not while our hellish friends are waiting for us outside.'

'When will they go?'

'When the sun comes up again. Why don't you try and get some sleep?'

Now it was Mouse's turn to roll his eyes at the horse. 'In a graveyard? With monsters outside the gates? And statues inside that whistle at me? Are you crazy?'

Nonky cocked her head thoughtfully to one side. 'Hmm. I'm a talking one-eyed horse in a little boy's story, looking for a mythical castle with a sheep and a robot dinosaur. *Am I crazy?* WHAT DO YOU THINK?'

Before Mouse could reply, Sir Dragnet clambered out of the grave. 'Hey, look at this, everybody! Look what I've found.'

At first Mouse couldn't quite see what the minstrel was holding. Trex was trying to lick it, but Dragnet pushed him away. As he got closer, Mouse blinked. He could see exactly what it was now, and wished he couldn't.

It was a skull. Cracked and dented, but definitely a human skull.

Mouse wriggled away as Sir Dragnet knelt down to present him with his trophy. Shuffling up against the gravestone, Mouse screamed at him.

'Get that away from me!'

Sir Dragnet shook his head kindly, while examining the piece of bone.

'What is it?' said Mouse. 'Is it a zombie? Is it . . . haunted?'

The minstrel looked up from under his floppy hat. 'No, sirrah. It is not a zombie, as you put it, or a spectre. It is just a skull.'

Mouse relaxed a bit, but still didn't dare go any nearer. 'It was somebody once though, wasn't it?'

Sir Dragnet nodded. 'Oh yes, it certainly was.'

He placed the skull softly on the ground, and Mouse steeled himself to take another look. It didn't shriek, no worm crawled out of the eye socket and it looked polished and smooth – not at all like something that had ever been an actual living person.

'Do you know who it was though?'

Sir Dragnet took the lute off his shoulder and crossed his legs, ready to play. 'I do, as it happens. Shall I tell you?'

Mouse looked up at Nonky, who for once didn't roll her eyes or tell the knight to shut up. He also caught sight of the hounds outside the graveyard, twisting their noses between the railings, sticking out tongues as black as liquorice. Perhaps just this time, after everything that had happened this evening, a minstrel's song would be nice. He nodded.

'Go on.'

In the waxy moonlight the minstrel began to pluck softly at the strings of his lute. Mouse noticed the furrows of worry in his brow, the burst veins in his cheeks, his blackened teeth and the way his hands shook slightly as they plied the instrument. He wondered if he would look that rough when he grew up.

Another thought struck him as well. Sir Dragnet reminded him very much of someone he had once known. Who though?

But he forgot all about it as the minstrel began to sing.

> He was just a man
> An ordinary man
> Just like you and me . . .

'Poor him,' snorted Nonky, but she didn't stop the song, and Dragnet continued, not missing a beat.

> He was just a man
> A very ordinary man
> He didn't rule the world
> Or reinvent the wheel
> He had holes in his socks
> Hairs in his nose and a touch of the pox
> He was just a man
> A very ordinary man

Mouse reached out for the skull – before he thought about the pox and changed his mind.

'Go on, he won't bite,' said Sir Dragnet. Mouse gingerly

picked the head up, noticing how heavy it was, as the minstrel started the next verse.

> *He bred pigeons, he grew roses*
> *A dad, and farmer too*
> *Who liked to jest or play a game*
> *No real claim to fame*
> *He didn't fly to outer space*
> *Not quite the master race*
> *More like an average guy*
> *Dumpy, frumpy, just a little shy*
> *No medals or trophies on his wall*
> *Unless you can win for being normal*
> *Don't get me wrong, he wasn't boring*
> *His family were adoring*

'And he wasn't the only one either,' said Sir Dragnet, wandering off with the lute.

'Really?' said Mouse, putting the skull down.

'Not at all. This place is full of ordinary folk, my lad.' He took out a filthy handkerchief from his pocket and polished the marble head of the whiskery gentleman who had given Mouse such a fright only minutes before.

> *Take a look at this hall of fame*
> *More like a walk of shame*
> *If this guy seems a prig*
> *Remember that he wore a wig*

It might have been Mouse's imagination, but the man's stone curls seemed to lift in a gust of wind, and a tinge of embarrassed flush rose up in his deathly cheeks. Next Dragnet passed behind the stark white statue of the young girl, frozen in the middle of her game.

> *This lass here, did she scare you?*
> *Have a heart now, don't be hasty*
> *She got swept off by the flu*
> *That's why she looks so pasty*

Suddenly, Mouse was less scared by the cold marble figure. In fact he felt sorry for her. Everywhere he looked, Dragnet had a line or a verse for the occupants of the churchyard. The angel with pointed wings was guarding the grave of somebody's gran. The knight brandishing a sword was a brave soldier, but he had died of a heart attack after eating too much Christmas pudding. There were people old and young, men, women, boys and girls – and as Dragnet sang, Mouse thought he could imagine the people behind the headstones and monuments.

Between two crumbling grey tablets he thought he spied two women, wearing coned hats on their head, with veils that drifted in the breeze. They nodded, and laughed at some private joke they were sharing. Over by the marble altar were more children, playing with a hoop and a small wheel spinning on a stick, shouting and laughing. One even held a small white pigeon in her hands, which flew off into the sky with a great flutter. There was a hunting party with dogs, knights and spears.

'But they all have one thing in common, old spark,' said Dragnet.

'What's that?' said Mouse, his eyes wide with wonder.

'They were ordinary folk.'

> *They lived like you and me*
> *Breathing, healthy and free –*

Nonky snorted again.

> *Peasants, jesters, queens*
> *People here of every means*
> *Death is not quite what it seems*
> *They lived like you and me*

They died like you and me . . . will
You can't escape the scythe
Whoever you are alive

He picked up the skull, and placed it carefully on the ground by the altar gravestone, like he was putting it back to sleep.

He was just a man though
An ordinary man
Just like you and me, y'know
Who wants to live forever?
I don't think that's clever
Death ain't nice but far from scary
It's everyday and ordinary
He was just a man
An ordinary man.

As Sir Dragnet plinked the last few chords on his lute, Mouse's eyes began to grow heavy. Perhaps it was his imagination, but he even thought the minstrel stroked his hair with his callused hand and covered him up with his tatty blanket. He was so tired, more tired than he could ever remember being in his life. The gravestones were cold but solid, and he slumped down against one of them. He knew he shouldn't go to sleep, something told him, but he just had to close his eyes for a few minutes – that was all.

Mouse never imagined in a thousand years that he would find it possible to sleep so comfortably in a graveyard, with the very worst terrors of the night waiting for him just outside. But as the spooks and nightmares faded from his mind, he closed his eyes at last and enjoyed the best night's rest he'd had in a very long while.

But only just along the valley from the churchyard, some other people were not getting any sleep at all.

And they were somewhere much more comfortable than a spooky graveyard. They were right on the top of a very steep hill, in a house converted from an old sheep barn. On this night, the farm where Granny and Gramps lived was reduced to just a pair of long windows staring out from under sagging eaves of snow, like a pair of frowning eyes beneath white bushy eyebrows. Strings of coloured Christmas lights dangled in front of each one, blinking brightly.

They were not the only flashing lights at the farm that Christmas Eve. There were also revolving blue lights on top of a police car, and red lights on an ambulance. In fact, the driveway was full of vehicles. The only problem for Granny and Gramps was that not one of them belonged to their daughter, or contained their grandchildren.

Inside the hall, a police constable stamped the wet snow from her shoes on to the mat, next to a row of wellington boots. She was still wearing a little Santa Claus badge she had been given at a children's centre Christmas party earlier in the day. Granny and Gramps's dog, a large golden retriever called Midas, came up, wiggling his behind and slurping at her hand. 'Hello, boy,' she said. 'Aren't you a handsome fellow, eh? Happy Christmas to you too.' She glanced at her watch and saw that it was, indeed, officially Christmas.

In the lounge next door, Mouse's grandfather was sitting in his favourite armchair by the old iron stove, lost in thought, his glasses perched on top of his head. As usual his chair was surrounded by piles of books, some splayed open, others covered in coffee rings and quite a few cracking apart at the spine. Not as usual though was the table in front of him. For once it had been cleared of the mess of papers that Gramps often let accumulate there, and instead various maps of the surrounding hills were opened out, weighed down by cups of tea. A local farmer was pointing at rivers and roads, saying things like, 'I've seen cars come off here before. You don't see that turn too well under the snow,' or asking questions. 'Did she come High Bratton way, do you know? Or would she normally take the main road through the valley?' A couple of other neighbours, dressed in the same mixture of quilted jackets and caps, with holes in their socks, were nodding and interjecting remarks about tractors and snow chains. From time to time one would take a sip of tea, and shake their head at it all.

If Gramps knew whether his daughter had taken the High Bratton way or not, he didn't show any sign. He didn't answer the question, but just turned his lined face towards the flames flickering behind the soot-singed door of the stove.

The questions had begun earlier that evening, at about seven, when there was still no reassuring growl of the SUV on the gravel outside. The door was yet to be flung open by children tumbling in with bags and presents. The box of toys they kept for the grandchildren had not been emptied all over the rug. No one was hugging his leg or pulling at his cardigan, asking ridiculous questions that could never be answered. The only person who was doing that was his wife, who asked the first difficult question of the evening, the one that was yet to be answered. 'Where do you think they could have got to?'

Nobody knew where they could have got to. Not the police, not the mountain rescue service, not Belinda's neighbours, and certainly not her ex-husband Derek, answering the phone blearily miles away in Florida; none of

163

them knew where Mrs Mallory and her three children had got to in the short drive between her house and theirs.

In the kitchen, Granny was meant to be making more tea for her guests. Not just the local farmers, but also a paramedic in a green boiler suit checking his phone, yet more police all the time, even the local child-protection officer. Granny wasn't actually making any tea though. She was standing motionless by the kettle, her hands gripping the worktop. No one knew where her daughter and grandchildren were. Their neighbours had seen them set off. The police had tracked down one witness, a lorry driver who had passed a black SUV matching the description of the Mallorys. But since then they had disappeared, off the face of the earth, it seemed. Her daughter was strong, but she was also the only adult among them. Violet was hugely practical of course. But little Esme was just a baby. And as for Mouse . . . Granny shuddered at the thought of her dreamy grandson being relied on in any kind of survival scenario.

Then came a voice, shattering her thoughts, summoning her into the other room.

Gramps, life back in his eyes, clutching his phone and hugging her.

'It's the police, my dear. They've only gone and picked up a signal from Mouse's phone, the clever beasts.'

164

The hillside was dotted with a confusing glimmer of lamplights, sweeping down across the snow.

But there was nothing confusing about the purpose of the searchers on the hills. The snowy verges were churned up by four-wheeled drives, emblazoned with fluorescent livery, aerials protruding from their roofs like upright lances. And they contained enough shovels, stretchers, oxygen cylinders and coils of rope to supply an expedition to Mount Everest.

From the verges, crisp boot tracks twisted up and down the slopes, while cries of 'Belinda! Violet! Esme! Mouse!' floated over the lights, interspersed with sharp toots from the whistles hanging around their necks. One or two of the rescue party – some thirty or forty strong – wore their hurriedly unwrapped Christmas scarves or gloves, a gesture to the family festivities they were set to miss.

It was so cold, bitterly cold.

The heavy weather was keeping any helicopters firmly on the ground. So the searchers were on their own. A collection of trained professionals and local volunteers, they were instantly recognisable in their matching waterproofs, coloured bright red like poppies. In their rucksacks they carried food, first-aid kits, maps, compasses and radio equipment. And several were being pulled along by search dogs. Border collies, at home in this kind of terrain – even in deep snow – sniffing for scent and barking as they dragged their handlers after them. Even in the torchlight, the black-and-white dogs occasionally seemed to disappear into the dark of night and the snow, as if they had been swallowed up by the land.

The dogs were following a scent they had picked up from a hat – a soft felt beret that Mrs Mallory had left at her parents'.

The police thought they had found something earlier – a trace of a mobile-phone signal, which had cut out after a moment or two. Not long enough to triangulate and trace; a sign of life perhaps, but only of a device, not necessarily a person, and nothing more. The area it could have come from was still huge. That was why they were all here, stamping their feet to stay warm in the early hours of Christmas morning.

'If they're here, we'll find 'em,' said Duty Inspector Carter. Inspector Carter was now officially Bronze Leader and in charge of the operation. The Mallorys did not merit a Silver Leader, because they were just one family reported as missing in the snow, not part of a larger party. If they had wanted a Gold Leader, they would have done better to be caught up in a national emergency. But Bronze it was, and David Carter was determined to find them. He had spent his working life serving the community in these moors and peaks, and had overseen the rescue of more fallen walkers, stranded skiers and trapped mountaineers than he could count.

His radio crackled and he sighed.

Unfortunately, it also seemed that every single person in Carsell had come out to look for the Mallorys. It was early on Christmas Day, and many grown-ups had not gone to bed, because they were keeping an eye on the sherry and biscuits left out for Santa, and many children were too wide awake and excited to sleep. Then the awful news of the Mallorys' disappearance had come through, pinging on dozens of mobile devices on bedside tables, their screens lighting up. A slightly confusing Facebook post by Gramps (who didn't use it very often) had gone viral and reached other parts of the globe hours before Father Christmas and his sleigh would.

As a result, the frozen and rutted track was thronged with neighbours in their onesies and fleeces, armed with everything from rakes to flasks of hot chocolate, desperate to help. A small posse of local police, in their high-vis jackets, tried hard to reason with them. But no matter how many times they had explained, no one would go home.

Inspector Carter shook his head. He didn't make the rules, the Health and Safety search protocols that said only trained rescuers could go out on the hills in these conditions.

'What I'm trying to explain, sir,' he had said, to one red-faced man in a Santa hat, 'is that it won't help save anyone if we let you endanger your lives. I can't even send my officers up there – it's trained search parties only, I'm afraid.'

'Nonsense!' blustered the man. 'I've lived here all my life. I know these hills like the back of my hand. It's a young woman and her children, can't you see?! Let us go, and we'll find them.'

But rules were rules, and Inspector Carter just folded his arms tightly in reply.

There was another reason of course, which he didn't tell the grumbling spectators, because it would only alarm them.

As the snow had stopped falling, every track would be fresh. The temperature was below freezing. The sensible thing for any stranded motorist to do (of course) would be to stay in their car, turning on the ignition at intervals to keep the heating on for short periods, keeping an eye on the fuel.

Unless, that is, any of them had decided to leave the safety of the car for some reason. Either way, the last thing the trained rescuers needed was a hundred other sets of footsteps across the snow, confusing the dogs and spoiling any tracks the missing persons may have left.

Inspector Carter shivered and stamped his feet. He was so absorbed in his own task, as he scanned the slopes opposite with his night binoculars, that he almost didn't hear the man next to him.

'If,' said Gramps, at last looking up from the soft beret crumpled in his hands, his glasses still perched on his head. 'You said, "*If* they're here."'

'Sorry,' said the policeman, misunderstanding him. 'Of course there's no if. They're here; we'll find them.'

'But, my dear chap, what if they're not here? Have you considered that?'

Inspector Carter turned to look at him, frowning from under the shadow of his snow-dusted cap.

'I don't follow. They have to be here. The main road from East Burn to your place comes through this valley. If she was driving the kids to you, they'll be down there somewhere, I'm

169

sure of it. It's just a matter of time, doctor. You know it is.'

Gramps shook his head impatiently.

'But I don't know it, old boy. Because one must also consider the possibility that they never got here in the first place.' His eyes were fierce, and a vein throbbed in the side of his grizzled head. 'You saw the storm that was blowing yesterday. In all my many years I have never seen the like of it. My daughter isn't a bad driver, she has known these roads for her entire life, and all that . . . but in the snow . . .' He stopped for a moment as a shout came down the line and there was a brief flurry of excitement . . . but it turned out to be nothing; a searcher had discovered some shiny wrapping paper stuck to a hawthorn bush, blown there by the wind.

The grandfather turned back to the policeman, convincing himself more and more with every crucial second that passed.

'What if, though, what if they never came into this valley to begin with? What if she took . . . a wrong turn in the blizzard and didn't realise?'

He glanced at the bobbled hats of spectators, the convoy of rescue vehicles, the lights of the search party flickering over the hillside like glow-worms.

'What if we're not even looking in the right place?'

The next day arrived long before Mouse felt ready for it. It was not even proper morning yet, but he could hear very distant noises – shouts and whistles – that woke him up, along with a stiff back, sore legs, and frost nibbling at his toes.

He wiped his eyes and yawned. The noises rose . . . and faded.

Where was he? Leaning against a gravestone, in a churchyard. For a moment he thought he was in there with his toys and an iPad, until he rubbed his eyes again and saw Nonky, Sir Dragnet (snoring noisily as he snuggled against Trex's belly) and Bar, who was busy marching around them all, bleating in a wake-up-let's-go kind of a way.

Slowly his friends got up, with lots of grumbling, scratching and stretching.

Nonky muttered about the need to get on, but there was absolutely no mention of breakfast or any kind of food. Not even a drink in fact. As Mouse put his armour back on, and strapped Wenceslas to his side, he wondered whether the minstrel might whip some bread and cheese out of his pouch. He ran his hands over the horse's armour, which shone dully in the grey dawn, hoping he might find some hidden saddlebags bulging with provisions.

But he didn't. Nor did Trex leap up and offer to go and catch them something to eat. Then, somehow, they were assembled and as ready as they were ever going to be.

Mouse wished his mum could have been there. She would have seen how quickly he could get up and ready in the morning when he really wanted to. Speaking of which, where was his mum? Before he could remember, they were facing the gate of the graveyard and he found himself thinking instead about what lay outside. He hesitated before clambering up on to Nonky's broad back.

'Chop-chop, Sir Bleary!' said the horse. 'Or I'll go without you.'

'But what about the hounds?' said Mouse, their red eyes and drooling jaws flashing into his mind.

'What hounds?'

'You know! Why are you being like this all the time?'

'Like what exactly?' said Nonky innocently.

'Treating me like I'm a stupid baby. Always being rude or pretending not to understand me, when I thought you were meant to be on my side.'

'I can't help my natural charm, can I? Anyway, take a look for yourself and see.'

The mighty charger nosed out under the arch. She sniffed the air, nodded and strode on to the hillside. Mouse recoiled, flinching as he expected the hounds to leap up and tear them to pieces.

Except they didn't – because in their place was a rock, a bush, and a hollow log, arranged in a haphazard semicircle outside the church railings. He didn't want to look too closely, in case they suddenly assumed their fiendish forms again, but they didn't. And there didn't appear to be a Pink Knight either. He might have retreated overnight, but Mouse doubted that he had gone very far.

But he also knew the castle could not be far away either.

Because there, opposite what remained of the hounds, were several smooth white boulders piled into a mound that came right up to his waist. This cairn was bigger and more impressive than the one by the well, and it filled him

173

with happiness because it meant he was right.

Cairns marked the way – a forest, a well and now a church. It was all coming back to him. Surely the next one would be by the castle itself, wouldn't it? He couldn't remember, but this cairn stood next to a gap in the railings. Perhaps if they walked through that gap . . .

Once they had left the church behind, gently picking a path along a ridge beyond, he asked the horse another question, one that he could no longer keep to himself. 'Who *is* that chasing us? The Pink Knight – who is he?'

'Well,' said Nonky, plodding along through some tall grasses that poked out of the snow, 'that all depends, I guess.'

'On what?'

'On whether you find the castle.'

The grass tips looked golden in the early-morning sun. Sir Dragnet found some winterberries, which he fed to Trex, who seemed to like them very much. Bar had quite disappeared apart from the points of her horns, and the occasional bleat, which suggested she was more than happy to be wandering through the deep snow and grass. She didn't seem worried about anything, just keen to eat as many stalks and leaves as she could in the shortest time possible.

However, Mouse was not a sheep or a dinosaur. He wasn't able to wander among the undergrowth and cheer himself up by stuffing his face. He couldn't forget the Pink Knight, or the slavering hounds of earth, or his experience of being in a grave. Between them they could only make him think of one, not very nice, thing.

'I don't want to die, Nonky,' he said. Trex growled behind them, and Mouse hastily added, 'I mean, I'm not scared of course. I just don't want to. Not yet. I'm too young. It's not right to die when you're only little, is it?'

'No,' said the horse, serious for once. 'It isn't right, not at all.'

'But are you frightened of dying?'

'I'm frightened of what I might do if you don't stop asking so many dumb questions.'

Mouse couldn't help but smile. It was weird, but he was getting used to Nonky being rude to him all the time. He almost . . . liked it.

They rode on, into the day. The sun began to rise properly in the sky behind the hills, lighting the whole valley up before them. But there was still no sign of a castle. It had to be nearby, surely? They had passed at least three of the cairns. Mouse was growing desperate for anything to make him forget about the clanking that he had once more started to hear behind them.

What he really wanted to do, though, was find something to eat. He asked the horse if they could stop for a bite, and she shook her jangling head. 'I'm afraid this is a non-stop service to the castle, sir. Let me just check in the galley to see whether we have any complementary pastries left.'

She paused, and Mouse felt the wind whistle past his ear.

'No,' said Nonky. 'I'm afraid we're clean out of complementary pastries this morning. We apologise for any inconvenience caused. Have a great day!'

'But I'm so hungry, Nonky.' And he was. He was really hungry. It was making him feel faint. Even though he wasn't doing the walking, it was effort just to stay upright while Nonky put one foot in front of another. Without meaning to, he began to slump slowly forward in the saddle.

'Which part of "no stopping" exactly do you not understand, sleepyhead?'

'I can't help it,' said Mouse. 'I've got no energy left.'

'Well, you'll have to help it, or—'

'Just five minutes, that's all.'

The horse clicked her teeth with irritation, and a few

steps later said, 'Jokes! Who knows any jokes? That's how we'll keep going. We'll tell some jokes.'

'I don't know any jokes, Nonky. I just want something to eat,' said Mouse. 'Please.'

'I wasn't asking you. Does anyone have any jokes?'

Ambling up alongside on Trex, Dragnet leaned over and pulled at Mouse's cheek, just the way his dad used to, which he had always hated. The minstrel spoke behind his hand as if he was telling a great secret, and his breath smelt of rotten Christmas-cake fruit.

'How about this one? You'll like this one. It's nice and short. What do you get if you cross a lion with a scorpion?'

'I don't know,' murmured Mouse weakly.

'Trouble both ends!' said Dragnet, shaking the bracelet of miniature cymbals around his wrist.

Mouse just closed his eyes.

'I had no idea that anything could be worse than your songs,' said Nonky. 'But, boy, you are nothing if not full of surprises, Dragnet. We mustn't let that boy pass out, whatever we do. Trex?'

'Meegh?' said the dinosaur.

'Yes, you, you overgrown automated fossil,' said the horse testily.

'Burgh I dorgh knurgh arry jogh,' said Trex. 'Eigh a dinosaurgh.'

'Well, think of one!' thundered Nonky. 'You've existed for sixty million years! Surely *somebody* must have told one joke in that time that you can remember. It doesn't even have to be good.'

The dinosaur plodded on for a few moments, Sir Dragnet sulking on his back, arms folded. Suddenly Trex pulled up short, nearly flinging the minstrel over his head.

'Eigh gurgh wun!' he said, sticking a claw in the air.

'This had better be good,' said the horse under her breath. 'Are you listening up there, dopey?'

Mouse's chin was buried firmly in his chest, but he muttered something that could have been a yes or a no; he really didn't care any more. He just wanted to curl up, to make his empty stomach stop cramping. Trex ploughed on regardless.

'Oh-hay,' he said. 'Whygh dig thurgh chickin croth thurgh roagh?'

Somehow, even though it was the last thing he felt like doing, Mouse managed to reply, speaking very slowly, 'I don't know, Trex, why did the chicken cross the road?'

'Becaugh thurgh dinosuargh wargh chathingh him!'

The dinosaur clutched his belly and laughed so much

that the spines on his back vibrated and the minstrel got a free massage. But Mouse's main reaction was a long strand of dribble that began to spool out of the corner of his mouth.

Then Bar, her stomach bursting with too many grasses of all kinds, came bounding up to overtake them and let loose her contribution to the joke competition.

Which was, quite simply, a massive fart.

It was no ordinary fart. In fact, Mouse wondered if it was the biggest fart that this sheep, or indeed any sheep, had ever released. This fart came out like a twelve-gun salute that had been made in the world's smallest lift, with the resulting explosion broadcast live on stadium-sized speakers. He imagined people fast asleep in their beds miles away getting up and going to the window, to see if they could spot the firework display that must have made such a racket. Or maybe, over in the next valley, there were two armies silently pitched on opposite slopes, waiting for battle, who each thought the opening shot had been fired and were now about to annihilate each other in spectacular fashion.

The fart was followed by a very short, stunned silence.

Mouse, who had been given the rudest awakening of all time, began to laugh. He chortled. He giggled so much that things sprayed out of his nose in different directions. Deep rumbles rose up from Trex in the closest a dinosaur can get to a belly laugh. Sir Dragnet tittered and even Nonky gave a few neighs in response. The only creature who didn't laugh at all was Bar, but she did look very relieved.

But then Mouse stopped laughing. 'Look,' he said, wiping the tears from his eyes.

The others were too busy guffawing and didn't hear him.

'Look!' he said again, more loudly this time.

They stopped laughing. They looked, and saw it too.

For there, poking up into the early-morning sky, just past the brow of a hill, were two spears lit by a golden light. As they drew closer, it became clear that the spears were the pinnacles of two slender towers.

They were the towers of a castle, shining in the dawn.

Mouse could see that the two spears – made of gold and lit by flaming torches below – were perched atop two tall towers of grey stone.

There may be a castle. Here was a castle.

It rose up from sheer cliffs in the distance, as if the walls and turrets and towers were just an extension of the rock below. The cliffs themselves were so high that bands of cloud covered the tallest pinnacles of the fortress. The towers were neatly encased in a square of crisp battlements.

How anyone would actually get up there was another matter.

Yet despite the winter fog drifting around it like a sea, this castle on the cliff was not grey and gloomy. It shone and shimmered. It looked as if it was made of sandstone or gold or glass, or some material yet to be discovered. Behind every battlement stood a flag. From every wall hung a banner. Richly embroidered lions, lambs, unicorns, swords, shields and flowers flapped in the breeze, fluttering and curling like sailing boats eager to take to the waves.

Mouse wished he could stretch his hand out and touch the walls to see if they were as solid as they looked. He wanted to plant his fingers in the arrow slits and pull himself up the walls. He wanted to tumble over the battlements and smell the cauldrons of boiling oil, get the dust from piles of straw in his nose and choke on the smoke of the great hall.

The whole party stopped with him to look on in wonder, gazing at the heralds in tabards who strode up and down, blowing their horns in the air. Out of the narrow windows, archers in helmets slid their bows. But they did not fire in anger. They sent showers of flaming arrows surging up into the sky, where they exploded in smoky puffs of phosphorescence, like fireworks.

And spread out around the bottom of the cliff was an encampment of tents, pavilions and stalls. Bright bunting was strung between the peaked tops of the tents and, below, the working day had already begun: butchers chopped meat hard on their blocks, porters tipped barrels of wet silver fish into trays of ice and grocers called out their wares in a steady song. Wealthy shoppers wrapped in wools and furs examined glittering objects spread out on cloths, or tasted cheeses from wandering sellers with trays. There was a falconer eliciting cries from a small crowd as his bird soared keenly in the sky, jesses tinkling, while puppeteers and wrestlers entertained on the ground. Ironsmiths pounded glowing anvils, swords were sharpened against millstones and pigs roasted on spits over fires, sending greasy clouds billowing into the air.

Even at this distance, it all seemed so close and real. It was as delicious as ice cream. It was a castle and a half. The most beautiful, magical, exciting, scary and strange castle he had ever seen. This is what they had been searching for, and it was just ahead of them now, on top of the cliff.

Mouse couldn't help himself. He punched his fist in the air and cheered. There was a castle. Nonky had been right. Everything was going to be OK. Stuff the Pink Knight and his scary hounds. The sheep was dancing around in a circle with Trex, and Dragnet was somehow strumming his lute with one hand while clinging to a dinosaur with the other.

A castle, a castle, a castle we can see
A castle, a castle, a castle we can see
A full-blown fairy fantasy

It's got towers and flags and sentries too
A king and queen, who wave adieu,
A castle, a castle, a castle we can see –

'Thank you, Dragnet, that'll be quite enough of that,' snapped Nonky.

For once Dragnet ignored the horse. And so did Mouse. He jumped off her back, and joined in the circle of Bar and Trex, jumping round and round to the minstrel's ear-shattering tunes.

Nonky didn't join in. She watched them all shouting and jigging, but there was no trace of a smile on her face. Slowly she turned about and clopped into the shade of a large oak tree, from where she stood and watched them. Her tail drooped, and her eyes softened as she watched the others play sword-fighting with Dragnet.

'What is it, Nonky?' Mouse ran to the horse's side. 'Come and play. We've found the castle! Just like you asked!'

'Yes, thank you,' muttered the horse. 'I may only

have one eye but I'm not blind.'

'So why are you being so boring?'

With a sigh, the great horse turned her head away from him. Mouse could not read her expression. But he noticed the single tear that welled up from deep inside her, rolling down her nose and on to the soft ground below.

He didn't understand.

Nonky was rude and mean. Nonky made sarcastic jokes and scoffed at everything. Nonky kept him going, even when he wanted to sit down in the middle of the track and cry. Yet now they had found what she had been nagging him to find all along, she didn't seem pleased or happy.

He looked up at her again, and in the horse's golden eyepatch he caught a glimpse of a child's face, reflected back at him as if from a shimmering pond.

And he realised.

'It's the castle. It's made you sad, hasn't it? Why did you want me to find it so badly if it was only going to make you cry?'

At first the horse couldn't reply, as if something was stuck in her throat. Mouse hugged her close, brushing off the clods of muddy snow.

'Finally,' said Nonky, her voice sounding cracked and strange. 'The first intelligent question you've asked.'

As Christmas Day began in the dark, Violet stirred from uneasy dreams into more confusion. She was no longer quite sure whether she was Violet, Captain O'Belty or Gráinne O'Malley.

She was past that.

She found herself sprawled across her mother, no longer caring about the gear stick prodding painfully into her side. Curled up on the same driver seat, clutching both her and their mother, was Esme, covered in the jumpers and coats Violet had finally managed to retrieve from the boot of the car.

Her stomach rumbled, her lips were dry and everything felt cold, even under the extra layers.

It wasn't fair.

Violet had tried hard at school. She had done her homework on time. Her exercise books were decorated with more gold stars than a royal planetarium and she regularly came top of her class in many subjects. She was learning to play the violin and her teacher was pleased with her progress. 'Keep up the practice,' he had said, 'and you might even get a distinction in your first exam.'

A distinction!

A violin player of distinction. Just imagine how that would make her mum glow with pride. But what use was that in a car with the fuel and battery slowly running out, the heater getting weaker and weaker, even as she turned the key on and off to ration the power? No exam mark was going to make her mother glow in the way she urgently needed to. Where was that power going to come from? Not from a perfect poetry recital in school assembly, that was for sure.

And yet . . . it hadn't been a waste of time, all that schoolwork, all that bending over books or hunching over a screen, being the first to wave a pencil in the air when a question was asked. It had given her Gráinne after all. Her befuddled and tired brain had somehow dug up vital snippets of information about life on ships: about conserving rations, huddling together to preserve warmth, and never separating, so that no one got lost overboard in a storm.

But they weren't on a pirate ship, not really. They were in a crashed car on the hills near home. The storm had passed. It was Christmas Day. And they were already separated. Mouse, thrown out of the car, and gone who knew where . . .

Violet didn't want to think too much about that. She couldn't bear to. She couldn't imagine a world without Mouse. Yes, he was infuriating. Always in his own world, lost to civilisation on some epic daydream, but he was ... Mouse. He was her brother. He had to be OK, didn't he?

But what if he wasn't?

'Right,' said Violet, pushing herself up stiffly from her mother. Mrs Mallory murmured something as she did. She looked even paler than before.

It only hardened her elder daughter's resolve.

She was tired of being the good girl. Always on time, always being responsible, keeping Mouse and Esme in check, helping her mum with *everything* after Dad left them.

Now they were stuck here in this deep freeze of a crashed car, in the middle of nowhere, with no phone signal. If anyone was looking for them, they were looking in the wrong place.

Would Gráinne O'Malley just lie here and wait to see what happened?

No. Gráinne O'Malley once dive-bombed an assailant

from the rigging of her own ship, a dagger between her teeth, to save the life of a crew member. That was the legend.

'It's a very exciting story. But are you sure it really happened?' Miss Wilkinson had asked kindly.

'Yes, miss,' insisted Violet. 'It said so on the Internet.'

Why did it matter if it was true or not? Gráinne's legend wasn't just an exciting story – it was an *amazing* one.

Violet didn't have any rigging, or even a cutlass. But she had a pair of wellies and a duffel coat with only two toggles missing. *Violet Mallory*, she said to herself, *you are not going to just sit there and take this. You are twelve and a half years old and nearly a teenager.*

The snow has stopped. You have smiling frogs on the toes of your boots and a sliver of cake in your pocket. You wrote a library project all by yourself about a pirate who never backed down. Your little brother is out there by himself, and he has never written so much as a word of a library project, because he is hopeless.

'Sorry, Mum,' she whispered. 'I have to go. For Mouse. But I'll be back as soon as I can with help, I promise.'

She took one last look at her mother and baby sister, locked together in a deep but chilly sleep. This worried her, although her mother did at least appear to have stopped bleeding. And as she covered them with one more coat, they

189

almost looked peaceful. Violet checked the heater was still running and gave both of them a kiss.

She clambered out through the back window with great care, so as not to cut herself on the broken glass, and began to march straight up the field, through the deep drifts of snow.

30

Mouse looked at Nonky. He couldn't understand why his question was so intelligent. He opened his mouth, but he realised he didn't know what to say now she seemed sad. His brow furrowed and he thought really hard about what she had just said. He didn't know what else to do. How did his mum try to cheer him up when he was sad?

He straightened his shoulders and slapped the massive horse's flank softly. 'Come on,' he said, in as deep a voice as he could manage. 'Cheer up. Whatever's making you sad can't be that bad, surely?'

Before Nonky could reply, there was a distant thud from the cliff-top, as the castle's drawbridge flopped down over the moat. They all turned to look.

Drums pounded from within, and a rider on a horse

clattered out over the planks, a cloak flapping behind him. He and his horse charged through the camp, past the steaming cooking pots, ducking under the lines of bunting, hurtling along a winding rocky path through the fog towards them.

Mouse put a hand on his sword, and Dragnet quickly stepped away from Trex, as the dinosaur began to swell, ready to greet the new arrival. The rider was now just a few furlongs away. A hunting horn dangled at his side, and a leather bag was slung over one shoulder. The horse – a skinny beast – skidded to a halt, and Mouse drew Wenceslas.

He had no intention of meeting any more Pink Knights unawares and wanted to be prepared. Trex growled, his shadow lengthening over the ground. Mouse worried that if the dinosaur became much bigger he might become uncontrollable.

The new arrival reminded him of someone. Was it his teacher? Except he couldn't imagine Mr Stanmore wearing a small burgundy pillbox hat, with an ermine cape, over a tabard and tights. The man dismounted and swept off his hat with an extravagant flourish, as he bowed so low that his balding head nearly scraped the ground.

So Mouse thought he should bow too.

The man bowed again.

Mouse bowed again.

The man bowed again.

Mouse bowed again.

Then the man bowed again – and Sir Dragnet coughed loudly.

Distracted, the man dropped his hat on the ground. Picking it up, he squashed it back on his head, and put his long copper horn to his lips. He tried to blow. He tried to blow three times, but only succeeded in making the noise of a balloon losing air very quickly. So instead he clapped his hands and stamped his feet.

'Our lookouts have spied you from our battlements. You can only be in this forsaken piece of country for one reason. Which brave knight among you seeks the castle?' he asked in a high, reedy voice.

Mouse looked at all the others, who urged him forward. 'I do.'

'May I see your risk assessment?'

'My what?'

'Your risk assessment,' said the man who looked like Mr Stanmore. 'Health and Safety. It can be very dangerous visiting a castle, you know.'

'I know,' said Mouse. 'There's this Pink Knight, and he

won't stop following us, and his beard grows and it kills everything—'

'We haven't got time for that kind of nonsense. Before approaching the castle, the relevant authorities require all visitors to complete this form in triplicate.' The man started rootling around in the leather pouch slung over his shoulder.

'What is all this, sirrah?' demanded Sir Dragnet. 'We are knights on an errand. We have no need of forms.'

'No form, no entry,' said the man. 'It's the rules. And I am Peter the Marshal, Herald of the King and Master of Arms.'

He thrust a very long scroll of paper into Mouse's hand, who began to read it.

NAME: NAME OF CASTLE

REASON FOR VISIT (delete where non-applicable)

BEARING GIFTS / JOUST OR TOURNAMENT / DECLARING WAR*

*See paragraph 155, subsection c below

LENGTH OF VISIT: **SIZE OF GROUP:**

Please confirm prior to your visit that you will not be carrying any dangerous or prohibited items from this list:
Sword, dagger, spear, mace, lance, poisoned ring, hammer, bucket of boiling oil, bananas.

'Bananas?' said Mouse, looking up. 'How are they dangerous?'

'The king's very allergic. Can't have them around,' said Peter the Marshal. 'Also, skins not properly disposed of can present a serious slipping hazard.'

Please enter the height of your horse to the nearest foot:
Does your horse conform to current safety standards?
Please enter your knight licence number here:

SWORDS AND WEAPONS

All swords and weapons must meet existing court safety standards. No sharp edges or points, in case of putting someone's eye out. Please use your weapon responsibly.
THE ASSOCIATED FEDERATION OF SWORDSMITHS AND SPEARMAKERS SPONSORS THIS MESSAGE.

HELMETS

Helmets must be worn at all times, including while in bed, in case of nightmares.

Please wear your helmet in the bath, in case of the water being too hot upon your head. Please wear your helmet outdoors, in case of flying catapults.

DRAGONS

Dragons are not permitted within the castle walls at any time.

'How about dinosaurs?' asked Mouse.

Peter the Marshal looked at Trex. The robot tyrannosaur had grown as tall as the oak tree behind them, eyes flashing, claws flexing. The marshal sighed. 'I'm afraid I would definitely have to classify him as a risk to Health and Safety.'

'Whargh healgh angh saghety?' asked Trex.

'The well-being of the citizens of the realm,' said the marshal.

'Yorgh meath I cargh eagh aggy og dem?' said the dinosaur, making a sad face.

'No, you absolutely can't eat any of them!'

'Orgh,' said Trex, downcast. 'Thag's a piggy. I light eagin cigichensh.'

While the health and safety officer and the dinosaur were having this confusing conversation, Mouse kept on unrolling the scroll. The more he unrolled, the longer the form became. He carried on reading until the paper piled up in rolls around his feet. It was far longer than any book Mouse had ever read. There were questions about his brain, his breathing and his heart. He had to tell them how much pocket money he got each week, and who from. (And then decide whether that question demonstrated consistent or inconsistent pronoun usage.) He had to tell them what books he had read and what his favourite television programme was. The form demanded to know what his results were in every subject. There were spelling and grammar tests, maths tests, and comprehension tests. Finally, it said:

DO YOU UNDERSTAND THIS QUESTION?

PLEASE ANSWER YES OR NO.

'What's the question?' Mouse asked the marshal.
'No help allowed!' the man snapped.
'But if I don't understand it, how can I answer?'

'That is the question,' said the man, as if to underline the point about not offering any help.

Mouse decided to come back to that one later, scratched his head and read on. He had to put in all his measurements, and the measurements of all his family members. He hesitated. Should he really put how small he was? Sometimes he hadn't been allowed on theme-park rides with the others because of his height. Why did they even need all this information? It was none of their business.

He hesitated again, trying to remember who the others were – the other family members. He knew he had some, but everything seemed covered by a fog as thick as the one around the castle above. It was hard to think clearly; that was the strangest thing about this land. It was easy to imagine things, lots of things, but it was hard to think straight in the way this form wanted him to.

He scanned through reams of more questions and tick-box statements:

I SWEAR THAT ALL THE ANSWERS ON THIS FORM ARE TRUE TO THE BEST OF MY KNOWLEDGE.

I HAVE NEVER DONE A BAD THING, SAID A CRUEL WORD OR HAD A NASTY THOUGHT ABOUT ANYONE.

I WASH MY HANDS FOUR TIMES A DAY AND HAVE NEVER WIPED MY NOSE ON MY SLEEVE.

I HAVE NEVER BEEN LATE FOR A LESSON OR ACCIDENTALLY STEPPED ON SOMEONE'S FOOT.

WHEN I GROW UP I WILL ALWAYS KEEP MY HOUSE IMMACULATE AND PARK MY HORSE IN THE CORRECT SPACE.

I WILL GET A PROPER JOB AND MAKE LOTS OF MONEY.

I WILL BE PERFECT IN EVERY WAY AND NEVER COMPLAIN ABOUT MY LOT.

The marshal could see that Mouse had nearly finished reading the form. 'Once you have completed this, you just need to get the minstrel, horse, dinosaur and sheep to fill one in as well.'

'I thought you said the dinosaur wasn't allowed in the castle?'

'He still needs to complete a form.'

Trex growled, and the marshal took a careful step back. But Mouse was no longer looking at the pile of paperwork or listening to anyone. A strange mist had descended over his eyes. For a moment he worried that the

Pink Knight had caught up with them.

Except for once there was no clanking or hissing to be heard.

He just suddenly felt very weak, like it was hard to stand up. His knees buckled, he sank to the ground and the world around him began to fade. It was as if the castle, its messenger, his friends and the fairy-tale countryside were all behind heavy glass. The cold he had felt at his back since being here was now everywhere, biting his fingers, frosting his eyelids, blistering his lips and burning his toes. What had made him feel this way? It was a reaction, as sudden and severe as an allergic attack. But he wasn't allergic to anything (certainly not bananas).

Dizzy, breathless and confused, he glanced down again at the giant pile of unrolled paper – which now came right up to his waist – and he realised the issue.

The words glared up at him through the fog in his eyes.

WHEN I GROW UP

Even the idea of such a thing seemed impossibly far away, like the castle. But Mouse realised, with a shudder, that if he took the time to fill in this whole form, answer all the questions – provide all the information asked, agree to all the rules, wait for a horse, a dinosaur, a minstrel and a sheep to do the same – it would be too late.

The Pink Knight and his hounds of earth would have caught up with them. His beard of destruction would have sucked the life out of them all.

They would never reach the castle.

He was always going to be little Mouse. He was never going to get older, bigger or in any way grow up.

Mouse stared at the scroll through the film of sadness forming over his eyes. It wasn't fair.

He wanted to grow up, more than anything else in the world.

There were so many things he wanted to do.

He wanted to learn to drive, and buy his own car. Then he could be on his own and listen to his adventure audiobooks in peace, without Violet saying they were boring (because they weren't adventurous *enough*).

Next he started thinking of all the other things he wanted to do. Dad had promised them a trip to Disneyland in the summer and he wanted to visit Raptor Encounter, and go to Universal Studios, where they had built a whole King Kong island. Dad said the burgers there were the biggest he had ever seen, and reckoned Mouse wouldn't be able to fit one into his mouth. Mouse wanted to prove him wrong. In fact he wanted to prove him wrong about lots of things. He was going to show Dad that he was good at school, even at the pointless things that no one ever needed in real life, like sums and spelling.

He wanted to learn to play the drums, the massive ones you only had to hit once or twice during the song.

Perhaps he was going to become really famous and have millions of followers, with everyone reposting his every word.

He could live in his dream mansion with a helicopter pad and a submarine base at the bottom, because his best friend Farouk had assured him that private jets were so yesterday, private submarines were the latest must-have for trillionaires.

But, Mouse remembered, he was going to give the rest of the money he made from being a superhero or playing the drums to charity – to help all the poor people and endangered animals in the world. As long as he could keep fifty or sixty million back for himself, that should cover everything else. Because he was going to build his mum a massive new house, rather than the rubbishy old-fashioned one she had to live in at the moment. It was going to have iris scanners that controlled the fridge, a voice-operated kettle, and a massive widescreen TV on every wall. She was going to love it! Apparently, in Japan they had invented a robot that could do the ironing, so Mum could put her feet up and watch her favourite telly shows all day long, even when he brought loads of dirty washing back home from his mansion.

He paused. Or perhaps there was a drone that would deliver that for him.

It didn't matter. These were details, which growing up would smooth out. He was jumping ahead.

There was so much. New chocolate bars to be designed, wars to be won, jokes to be shared and cool things to be seen. He wanted to tour the wonders of the world – to go to every location of every James Bond film ever made for starters. Maybe even go into space. Farouk said that by the time they were grown-up, you would probably be able to get a bus there from the end of the road.

So much to do, to say, to see.

But if he filled in all of this form, never mind whether he even got the answers right, he would never get to the castle before the knight caught them. He didn't exactly know if getting to the castle equalled growing up, but he felt it had to be related, it was so important. And what could be more important than growing up, being who you wanted to be and no one being the boss of you?

Sighing, he glanced down at the roll of paper in his hands again.

And jumped. Half of the form was missing.

The bottom half had completely vanished, and the top half was disappearing fast.

Into Bar's mouth.

Her eyes closed in blissful contentment, the sheep was devouring Peter the Marshal's Health and Safety Form, munching her way through the juicy rolls of paper which dangled from Mouse's hands.

Munch, munch, munch.

Everyone watched in horror as she chomped and chomped, before gobbling up the last scraps from his empty palms. She licked her lips with her big sheep tongue, opened her mouth and gave a belch so loud that behind them a squirrel fell out of a tree. Bar just bleated a couple of times, in a those-forms-were-delicious-have-you-got-any-more kind of a way.

'You stupid sheep!' said Mouse, standing up so fast that Bar shied away in panic. He caught himself. How was she to know that eating forms was a bad thing? She was a sheep. 'Now we'll never get to the castle, you see,' he added, trying to sound more gentle, but it was hard to hide the desperation in his voice.

'Yes,' said Peter the Marshal, sneering down his pointed nose, which looked sharp enough to pierce any balloon, 'only one form per castle entrant, I'm afraid. No spares, no duplicates, no blanks, no retakes, no rewrites. Life is not a rehearsal. One chance and that's your lot.' He smiled, but it wasn't a nice smile. It was the kind that made you feel a little bit sick inside. 'Oh well,' he said, rubbing his hands together, 'never mind. Enjoy the rest of your day.'

He turned around to remount his scrawny nag, but something yanked him back.

It was a large hoof, treading on the hem of his fancy ermine cloak.

'That's not quite true, is it, my lord marshal?' said Nonky, who had been quiet for much of this conversation.

'What do you know about it?' snapped Peter, rubbing his neck. 'You're just a horse.'

'Maybe,' said Nonky. 'But I still know the rules.'

Peter looked down at his polished boots. 'I don't know what you're talking about. No one does that any more. Everyone prefers to fill in that form. It's much easier. Much safer, no one gets hurt, everything is controlled and orderly.'

'But there might be another way to get into the castle?' said Mouse, his eyes lighting up.

'Maybe,' muttered the marshal.

'*Definitely*,' said Nonky.

'Tell me what it is,' said Mouse, stepping forward.

The marshal scowled and waved him away. 'Trust me, you don't want to know. Not suitable for young boys at all.'

'Tell me!'

'For Gawd's sake,' interjected Sir Dragnet, 'put the lad out of his misery, me old china, or I'll play yer a ditty.' He started strumming his lute.

> *There was an old marshal called Peter*
> *Whose breath really could've been sweeter*
> *But he only ate onions with mice*
> *Which put paid to his words smelling nice!*

'All right, all right!' said the marshal. 'There is another way to enter the castle. But I have to warn you, it is very, very dangerous indeed.'

'Oh, guggy!' said Trex, his jointed tail thumping the ground. Everyone gathered round to hear, including Bar, whose horns twisted in with curiosity.

The little man stepped forward and poked Mouse in the chest. 'By the power invested in me, I invite you to accept the King's Challenge.'

'What's the King's Challenge?'

'Any persons wishing to enter the castle without first completing the required documentation must instead defeat the king's champion, at a tourney.'

Mouse looked at him blankly. He had no idea what a tourney was.

'Jousting, sunshine,' said Dragnet, clapping him on the back. 'It's a right royal battle of the lances and no mistake. Whomsoever leaves the field last goes over the drawbridge, innit.'

Finally, for the first time in a very long time, Mouse gave a big smile – nearly twice the size of his face – and actually meant it.

Because if there was one thing he was really, really good at, it was jousting.

32

Violet had climbed up the hill from the car, back towards the road. Thick cloud obscured any light from the moon or stars. The snow-covered countryside was like an old carving in an unlit corner of a church. Dark curves and shiny edges – but it was hard to make out exactly what anything was without going closer. And she didn't want to leave the safety of the blank white field. She had no idea where they were.

In fact, had it not been for the bright torch beam from Mouse's phone, Violet thought, she probably would have turned back after two minutes and climbed straight back into the car. At least Esme's insistent craving for chocolate had been some use after all.

She cast the torch back and forth across the ground, desperately looking for footprints, but there had been so much snow it was hard to see if there were any at all. Just before the road, though, next to the close-wedged print of a sheep, she saw marks that looked like the squashed imprint of a wellington boot.

The tracks continued for a while along the ridge of the valley, below the road, and then disappeared into nothing. Was it possible that he hadn't taken the road? Violet shivered. Her duffel coat was warm, and she was sensibly wrapped up in a woolly hat, gloves and a scarf. But still the cold cut right through. You couldn't escape it.

Even with the bright light from the torch, nothing looked familiar in the darkness – the shape of the hills, the valley ridge, the curve of the road – this wasn't anywhere she recognised from the usual way to Granny and Gramps's.

Perhaps it was just different at night – that was it – and the snow was confusing her.

Looking behind her, down the hill, she could still just make out the glinting crumpled wreck of the car. There were rows of pine trees behind the wall. A forest. It might be the one Dad had nicknamed the Haunted Forest, but that spread for miles through the valley.

She paused at the point on the path where the sheep and boot tracks had been recently covered by a fresh fall, looking at the smooth and reassuring dark curve of the snow-caked road just above, and considered her options once more. What had Mouse done here? Had he known where he was? That seemed unlikely.

This was harder than she had expected. For one thing, she hadn't thought she'd be quite so tired and so very hungry. Of course she had done the right thing, left most of the cake for Mum and Esme. Mum was bound to wake up soon, surely, and then she would look after them both and keep an eye on the engine. But that left little food for her to take on her expedition, and she had eaten half of that already.

It didn't feel like she had been walking for that long, but the valley was so steep, the temperature so low, that both the terrain and the climate had sucked every last molecule of energy out of her. She felt dizzy, and on several occasions had to lean against a tree or sit down on a rock. And each time getting up again was harder.

She should not have left Mum and Esme in the car.

But *Mouse*. But getting help. But . . . lots of things.

Violet held her brother's phone with the torch out towards the horizon ahead, straining her eyes, desperately searching for any clues. But the beam didn't reach far enough to help. So she checked for any mobile signal again, just in case.

Nothing.

She turned it off for a moment.

Immediately the world felt a colder and scarier place.

But, as her eyes adjusted to the very faint light beginning to creep up over the horizon, and she stamped and clutched her arms and shivered, Violet thought she saw something she recognised.

What was that — right over there — a single silhouette against the approaching dawn? A tree that didn't have any branches? A tower?

No. It wasn't a tree or a tower.

It was a chimney, or at least the remains of an old one. A flue from the old lead mines, sticking up out of the moors. Not just any old chimney though. It was a sign — the first piece of good news after a long, cold and scary night.

At last she had found a clue — a landmark on the way to her grandparents' house at Carsell. But a landmark that looked miles away. Had Mum taken a different route to normal? Violet wondered if they were even in the right valley. Would Mouse seriously choose to walk all the way there, from here, in this weather? That seemed a very poor choice in every way.

Yes, Violet decided, that was just the kind of thing her brother would do.

She glanced at her watch as she skidded down the hillside,

away from the road, towards the distant chimney. How could she forget? Christmas Day was beginning, and she was going to make it happy for everyone.

She was.

Mouse studied the new instructions the marshal had left. Even though this was a different way to enter the castle, there were still fresh forms to fill in, which Bar was already eyeing up greedily. And this paperwork could not have been clearer.

Anyone wishing to enter the castle without completing the risk assessment had to prove their worth by defeating the king's challenger. This wouldn't be the king himself, of course, because it turned out that he was as allergic to physical combat as he was to bananas – if not more so.

Mouse still felt cocky when he read this, because it sounded as if the owner of the castle was more of a scaredy-cat than a scary king. Although he did feel a small twinge of suspicion when Nonky explained that that meant he

214

would have to face one of the king's top knights. 'Don't worry. He will probably just be the strongest and fastest jouster in the land, with an undefeated record, and thousands of loyal fans cheering him on from the stands. It'll be a piece of cake.'

If that was a piece of cake, thought Mouse, it sounded like quite a frightening sort of cake. He suddenly felt rather less cocky. Yes, he was really, really good at jousting IN A COMPUTER GAME. Top of the leader board seven times, and he had beaten Farouk eighteen times in a row.

But – he realised with terror – this was not jousting on an iPad; this was jousting in real life. The lances he knew how to dodge were made of pixels and operated by code. The ones he had just agreed to face would be made of iron and timber, and he was made of flesh and bone, last time he checked.

Suddenly he wanted to be anywhere but here. Where was here, anyway? This land of haunted forests and high cliffs, inhabited by dinosaurs that lived in wells and talking horses who were on Instagram. It all felt too much like a dream. Strange things kept happening, and changing, going round and round in his mind. He couldn't seem to control or stop any of these events, yet at the same time felt sure they were all somehow linked to his own thoughts.

It reminded him of the time he got the flu and was off school for a week. By the end, he was well enough to watch Netflix on his tablet, but at the beginning he had a fever and his mum kept coming into his room with a thermometer to check his temperature. His dreams had been beyond weird, and they had merged with his waking thoughts and he couldn't always tell where he was or who was in his bedroom. He remembered having a dream about werewolves, and when he woke up the werewolves only half disappeared. The light was on, he was in his bedroom, but they were still in his head and didn't go away until his mother gave him another dose of Calpol.

And all this – Nonky, the joust, Trex – was like the werewolves.

He didn't know what was going on any more. The others were distracted, poring over the scroll of parchment Peter the Marshal had given them. Bar was trying to eat it, while Dragnet argued with Nonky over what colours Mouse should wear. Trex was scratching his head, asking why anyone needed to fight, when he could just eat the challenger in a single gulp, but the rules didn't allow for that.

What colours he should wear – red and white, or blue and gold – what did that matter? What did *any* of it matter?

If this joust went ahead, only one thing was certain. He would get badly hurt, or worse. Much worse.

That was the most frightening thought ever. Mouse didn't know what to do about it. He couldn't show Nonky – and certainly not Trex – that he was scared. He couldn't talk to Dragnet or Bar – that would just be embarrassing, for all of them.

So Mouse started to run.

Violet could go no further. It had started to snow again. She had never wanted a white Christmas less. She had made it to the old chimney, and had already decided that was a walk she never ever wanted to do again – especially in snow and on an empty stomach. Dad had always told them to steer clear of the chimney anyway, because of dangerous chemicals in the ground left behind by the lead mining. He said if you breathed in too many of the fumes, it could do funny things to your head, like causing hallucinations.

Only Violet wasn't hallucinating. The tracks of sheep and boy had long disappeared, but she had just found something better.

Christmas cake. She thought she had been imagining it at first, a little trail of crumbs in the snow. But there was no mistaking this. It wasn't a scattering of pebbles or seeds. It was definitely Christmas cake. The one they had all made with their mum.

Mouse had been here. Somehow he knew or had found the way. Violet poked at the crumbs with her boot. Had he left the trail on purpose or by accident?

It was a clue for sure, but she didn't know if she had the energy to follow it up. She was so tired. Maybe it was the fumes, maybe hunger, maybe the cold, but Violet couldn't stop herself collapsing against the ruined walls of the flue. Her hands looked whiter than snow, and her head was swimming with emptiness. It was as if she could float away at any second. Curling her arms around the chimney, she wished for it to be warm in a way that it just wasn't as she stared out across the valley into the snow that began to fall again, in little eddies, like cotton blossom caught by the wind.

It was becoming possible to make out the blurred outlines of the landscape ahead, the features she dimly recognised from the times they had all done this walk together.

How had Mouse got this far, in the dark, in this cold? He didn't even have the torch from his phone to guide him. Unless he had taken the iPad, but why would you take an iPad on a walk?

It seemed . . . impossible.

Yet there was that Christmas cake dropped at her feet.

Violet scooped up a handful of the crumbs and gobbled them up. They were frosty and damp, but it very definitely tasted of cake. Not just any cake, but all the flavours they had mixed in together – dried fruit, candied peel and almonds – in the kitchen at East Burn. The cake tasted of home, of family.

The family who were all still out there.

Violet put on her best Gráinne O'Malley grimace and pulled herself up, grabbing at the flaking stones of the chimney. As she did, she caught sight, through the billowing snow, of a single black spire poking up between the hills ahead.

Granny and Gramps's local church, the tiny one miles from anywhere, where they sometimes went on Christmas Day. The Church of the Holy Trinity – or as they all called it, because the heaters never worked, the Church of No Electricity.

Their house was in the next valley along, on top of that steep hill. So near! Her heart began to race as she imagined the warm glow behind the condensation in the windows, the shuffle of her grandma's feet as she came to answer the door –

And yet, the wind was so biting. The cold stung her lips and eyes. There were miles left to walk, and all she wanted to do was find a large boulder, curl up behind it and go to sleep.

Violet tugged the layers of dressing gown and winter coat even tighter around her, and for the forty-fifth time that morning asked herself what Gráinne would do.

In the story of her life, she had read that once O'Malley stood on the bow of her ship, in a storm, her eyes fierce and her hair flying, not afraid, whatever weather, sea or enemy might throw at her.

Her most devoted disciple marched on through the drifts.

35

'Wait!' shouted Nonky after him, but Mouse didn't care.

The whole thing was pointless. He was never going to defeat the best knight in the land. If anything, he would end up hurt – or even killed. No one had actually explained what was so special about this castle anyway. Mouse and his family had once been to a castle in Wales. There were holes where the windows should have been, and grass growing over everything. The floors, walls and roofs had crumbled away. Apart from some peeling laminated info boards and a few mouldy flags, there hadn't been much to get excited about.

More than anything, he just wanted to go home.

He was tired of this journey. Cold, tired and hungry, not to mention bored. It was time to go home.

If only he could remember where that was.

Mouse stopped and looked around. He had been running for a while, swishing his way up the slope from the cliff and the castle, through rotting bracken, stumbling over rocks. He had no idea where he was, or where any of his friends or the castle now were. A low mist had settled in around him, floating over the trees and hills. His skin felt wet and clammy. Everything had gone very quiet, apart from the odd harsh cry of some bird – a crow perhaps.

It was the middle of nowhere, and yet somehow he felt he wasn't alone.

Mouse closed his eyes and listened really hard. He could hear his own heart, his lungs breathing in and out, and tried to imagine the rest of his insides whirring like clockwork. He could hear his own body in minute, piercing detail, but he couldn't hear anything else. Not even a blade of grass stirred in this damp fog.

He wanted it all to go away. But some instinct made him open his eyes again. And out of the corner of one, he thought he saw –

An owl, sitting on a tree stump, that rose out of the mist ahead.

Mouse blinked. The bird reminded him of someone,

but who, he couldn't quite remember. It waved at him with its wing.

'Toodle-oo!' it said.

'Hello!' called Mouse back. He was getting used to talking to a horse or a dinosaur, why not a bird too?

'I say, old boy,' said the owl, waving at him, 'any chance you could lend a chap a hand?'

This was a very strange owl. But Mouse was finding it harder and harder to speak, his teeth were chattering so much. If only there was someone who could lend him a jumper or a hat.

'Toodle-oo! I say, old fruit, are you completely deaf? I'm over here.'

Warily, Mouse walked over. As he got closer, he saw that the owl was quite a fat one, and old too, judging by the number of grey feathers. It was also the first owl Mouse had ever seen with a pair of gold-rimmed spectacles perched on its head.

'You're terribly kind,' said the owl. 'Would you mind giving me a hand? Awfully embarrassing, but I seem to have got my whatsit stuck in the thingummy.' He pointed down at the tree stump. Mouse looked, and as he got closer saw that the owl was wearing a very long gown, about eight sizes too big, which had got twisted right round the roots of the tree – like a rag caught in a propeller.

'It's completely hopeless,' muttered the bird. 'Sixty thousand spells in this old noggin and not one of them designed to free the hem of a robe from a tree. And in my . . . well, you can see how it is,' he said, flapping his wings uselessly.

'You're stuck,' said Mouse.

'I can see I'm going to have to watch you,' said the owl. 'You're quite the detective.'

Mouse crouched down and began to work the robe free.

'Oh, capital, my dear fellow, absolutely capital. If you could try your very best not to tear it, I would be most obliged. This robe was given to me by Cleopatra herself, y'know.'

'Right,' said Mouse, nodding and beginning to wonder how soon it would be polite to make his excuses. This owl was madder than his music teacher, Mr Thackthwaite, and Mr Thackthwaite liked to put marmalade in his sausage sandwiches.

It was, though, a very beautiful robe.

The material was soft in his hands, but so thin he worried he could tear it at any moment. Looking at it, he was reminded of some of the curtains and cushions in his grandparents' house, the ones they had to be careful with and on no account spill anything on. The robe was embroidered with expensive-looking patterns, which caught the light as he tried to pull the fabric loose. There were distant suns, planets, moons, circling in orbit around the hem of this strange bird's gown. Pyramids, palm trees and whales. Not to mention castles, trains and spaceships. Robots, just like on his pyjamas, monsters and dinosaurs. It showed every animal in the jungle, every fish in the sea, a map of every forest and lake in the world. The gown seemed to stretch on for ever and ever, running through his fingers like water. Finally, with a gentle tug, it came free.

Mouse stood up, looking at the owl's great tufting eyebrows. He looked so old. Beneath, his eyes were full of sadness.

'Who are you?' he said.

'I am . . .' the owl began, 'very forgetful! I say, if you could be so kind as to pick me up . . . mind the robe . . . gently does it, I'm over a billion years old my dear chap . . . and if you also wouldn't mind stretching down to grab that . . .'

Cradling the bird carefully against his chest, as he had seen his mother do with Esme, Mouse crouched down and picked up what looked like an old blue bag.

Only it wasn't a bag.

It was a large conical hat, crooked at the tip, with a wide floppy brim. The hat was made of a velvety felt the colour of a midnight sky, one that glittered with a thousand silver stars. Mouse felt a glow of relief and understanding. Finally something he recognised without question.

A wizard's hat.

36

Mouse followed the owl's directions, slipping and sliding over loose stones, until they came to a shadowy opening that seemed to lead inside the hill itself.

He had to pick his way around tottering piles of tatty books, their dog-eared covers flapping in the breeze, bubbling pots overflowing with mysterious steaming liquids and a desk buried under scrolls of parchment, that toppled on to the floor with a clatter as they brushed past.

'Oh, fiddle,' said the owl. 'It took me two thousand years to get those in order. Never mind. Now where did I . . . ?' He squinted up at Mouse in the gloom, the spectacles still perched on top of his feathery head. 'Where did you put my glasses, dear boy? You really must stop playing these ridiculous games, it's quite . . . oh, blast . . .'

Mouse unhooked the owl's wings from around his neck and sat him carefully down on what looked like a rug made from a giant tiger.

'Ah, the sabre-tooth, excellent choice, monsieur,' said the owl, padding around the fur on his claws. Then, glancing at his guest's dumbfounded face, he added hastily, 'Oh! Not what you think! I wouldn't touch a hair on his head . . . this one's mother gave me his pelt as a gift after he passed away. Very sad. He was a terribly keen reader, you know. Not too many reading tigers about these days, more's the pity. When *was* that?' He started to count on his wingtips. 'Last Tuesday? Or last millennia? Ah well.'

Mouse sat down beside him. There seemed to be some sort of stove by the rug, like the one in his grandparents' house, but it was ice cold to the touch and clearly hadn't been lit in a very long time. He considered asking where some logs or the matches were, before looking around the cave – which really was like one of those junk shops his mum sometimes enjoyed poking about in on holidays – and thinking better of it. How would he ever find matches under that pile of furniture or those mirrors stacked against the wall?

'Who are you?' he asked again. And this time he really meant it.

The owl flicked his wings and the stove crackled into life. 'I am . . .' he began and then sighed. 'I am very, very old, is what I am. But who I am . . .' He glanced sharply at Mouse and his wide yellow eyes flashed jet black. When he spoke next, his voice echoed around the cave, as if coming from far beneath the earth. The words had a reverberating hollowness, a sharp tang that they did not before. The sound seemed barely animal or human. His chest puffed up and he suddenly seemed a much bigger owl, his outspread wings casting giant shadows on the walls in the light of the stove. 'I am the guardian at the gate, the eyes under the earth. By a deeper magic sired, at the wrong end of time. As the moon wanes, so I grow younger still, yet under these rocks perforce lie I until my king returns.' The owl sank back on to the tiger-skin rug with a little sigh. His voice lost its supernatural echo, but still sounded ragged and elderly. 'I am . . . whoever you want me to be.'

Next there was a strange sucking, popping noise, and the owl transformed in front of his eyes into a very old man with a white beard, sucking on a pipe. 'I can be this, or this.'

POP!

The old man turned into a frog, leaping about the rug, perching on the sorcerer's hat like it was a rock in a river. 'Or this?'

POP!

In a flash the frog vanished, and a huge crouching beast filled the cave. It was covered with shaggy dark hair, and its many thick feet were clawed. The creature's eyes were distant suns in the night of the cavern, and it wielded a club the size of a small tree.

'No!' gasped Mouse, shrinking back. 'Not that!'

POP!

'Or maybe even this?'

All trace of the frightening monster vanished, and in its place sat the owl again, scratching his head. 'Oh, dearie me, I'm sorry about that. Transformation can be terribly difficult sometimes . . . I really don't know where that horror came from. That's what comes from attempting magic on an empty stomach.' He rubbed his big owl belly. 'I'm absolutely famished. How about you?'

'Yes,' said Mouse. 'Starving. What did you say your name was again?'

'Oh, just call me . . . I say, will you look at that!' The owl pointed into the depths of the cave, where something was beginning to stir. Mouse hoped it wasn't another hairy beast.

It was something shining in the dark. But this time the shiny thing turned out to be a copper cauldron skipping towards them. The copper cauldron was followed by a large toasting fork and a sparkling knife. They marched towards the pair and around them. Soon they were joined by a mouth-watering steak, a pair of sausages doing the can-can and a whole troupe of acrobatic roast potatoes rolling in formation. Pitchers of milk waltzed with wobbling towers of fudge cake. Even some vegetables got in on the act, with big juicy branches of broccoli doing what looked like a Scottish reel with a few nervous-looking carrots.

Mouse's jaw fell wide open, and the owl seemed to fade from view, as golden plates, crystal goblets and silk napkins paraded around them and the assorted lines of food, crockery and cutlery moved faster and faster, wheeling high into the air.

Mouse rubbed his eyes.

The cave was dark and cold once more. Staring at him, with his wrinkled and bloodshot eyes full of kindness, was the old man the owl had turned into, a pair of glasses perched upon his pink nose. He rubbed his long beard thoughtfully and didn't say anything. Neither did Mouse. He was still eating delicious imaginary food off golden plates. For a moment he no longer felt tired or hungry or scared. Just for a moment.

'So, why did you come to see me?' said the wizard.

'I didn't,' said Mouse, still in a daze. 'I was nervous about this fight I have to do, and I . . .'

'Didn't want to let the others know you were scared?'

Mouse nodded.

'Are you still scared?'

'No . . . I mean, a bit, yes.'

'What are you most scared of?'

'I don't know. Everything really. I've only done pretend jousting on my iPad, and they're going to get the best jouster in the kingdom to fight me. What if he attacks me with a sword?'

The wizard leaned forward, his eyes narrowing, staring intently at Mouse, who felt as if the old man was looking right inside his mind. 'Well, what then?'

'I don't want to get killed!'

The old man shrugged. 'I see your point, but when you've been killed as many times as I have . . .'

Mouse kicked out at the pile of junk around them in frustration. An old chair without a seat toppled backwards and hit a grandfather clock. 'It's different for you! You're not a boy. Also, you're not . . .' He faltered, searching for the right word.

'*Real?*' suggested the wizard, arching a bushy eyebrow at him.

'Yes,' said Mouse. 'You're not . . . real.'

'And if I'm not real, then by logical extension, is any of this – real?' The wizard's voice had become dark and echoey again. He waved his cloak, wrapping it around Mouse. In an instant they were no longer in the cave of junk, but flying out over the land he had just travelled across, carried by scrolls of cloud. He looked back at the cave they had left, and he remembered someone once talking about a wizard's cave. It had been far away, in a distant hillside, and now he had found it. Next they were right back over the field near the Haunted Forest where he had woken up, then at the glade by the Well of Doom, and the graveyard and then by the oak tree at the bottom of the cliff where he had left his friends; he saw them still gathered around in a circle. 'Are *they* real?'

'I don't know! It's different . . . They feel real, somehow.'

'Well – you have your answer.' They were back in the cave again, and the wizard was pouring tea from a brown china pot with a cracked spout. 'Scone?' he said, offering Mouse a mountain of the butteriest, creamiest, jammiest scones he had ever seen.

Mouse took one, and a large bite, chewing thoughtfully for a minute. 'You mean, if it *feels* real, then it might as well be real?'

The wizard didn't say anything, but somehow pulled out the largest scone from the bottom of the pile, without making the others collapse. 'Bingo!' he murmured to himself, wolfing most of it down in one bite.

'That is quite weird,' said Mouse. It reminded him of the time Farouk had tried to explain the meaning of life. Farouk insisted that neither he nor his classmates existed, that they were only animated pixels randomly generated by an alien supercomputer for its own amusement (which in turn was just animated pixels randomly generated by an even bigger supercomputer for its own amusement, which in turn . . .).

'Not particularly. It's called the imagination. Imagine *not* having an imagination – that would be weird.' His lined face frowned at the thought.

'So all this, everything that's happened to me, has come from my imagination,' said Mouse, his eyes widening.

'I know,' said the wizard, flicking crumbs off his lap. 'You ought to get that looked at.' The crumbs rolled together on the floor into a scone crumb sculpture of a kindly doctor with a stethoscope, who held the instrument against Mouse's head and sighed, before exploding in a floury puff.

'Which means I might only imagine dying?'

'That is the most anyone can ever do, if you think about it.'

Mouse thought about it, and thought about it some more. 'Because if you really are dead, you can't remember it, or tell anyone what happened? So you can only imagine it? Even if I do die in the end.'

The wizard stood up. His sleeves were long and dragged along the ground. 'Please, no more talk of dying. Not just after my first scone of the day. Aren't there adventures to be had? Hearts to be won, knights to be vanquished, castles to be gained?'

Mouse stood up. It was hard to explain, but he felt stronger somehow. Everything felt clearer. Not easier, or nicer, but simpler. There was just one thing though.

'But . . . why am I imagining all this? Is there a reason?'

The elderly man looked across to the mouth of his cave in the frozen hills. Mouse wondered which was older – the hills or the wizard. A stark white light caught his profile, the contours and canyons of his ancient face, a few dots of snow blowing in on an icy blast. At that moment, he didn't look imaginary at all. He looked old and tired, and sad.

'Oh yes, there is most definitely a reason. Three of them in fact.'

Finally at the church, Violet slumped against the railings, heaving for breath. Down at her feet, opposite the cairn, she noticed a log, a stone and a small uprooted bush, arranged in a semicircle on the snow. Almost as if someone had put them there on purpose, which was odd.

Mouse. Was it another sign, like the crumbs, that Mouse had been here?

Turning around, she looked instead at the church. It stood cold and dark and empty. Perhaps she had already missed the early-morning service, the one they never made it to, and that only a few people in the village ever attended. But maybe the vicar or somebody might still be in there? Violet had stayed behind once to help tidy away prayer books and watched while one of her grandmother's friends had carefully

237

watered all the winter flowers. She began to pick her way up the slippery black flagstones towards the heavy oak door, trying not to look at the graves either side of her, with their crooked and frightening shadows.

Her hand paused on the iron ring, dangling from the door. It sounded too quiet inside. What if someone was praying? What if the door made a noise and the priest turned around and shushed her? It didn't matter. This was an emergency.

The door swung open with a creak, dragging over the worn grey stone. There was no one praying, no one there at all. There was just an empty church, smelling of beeswax and dust. In the blue light she could just make out the dark pew backs, and a single tapestry on the wall that looked ready to curl up and go somewhere warm for its holidays.

Violet coughed, and the noise ricocheted round the empty chapel. It felt hard and lonely. The last time she had been here, there had been candles and music, and other children wearing paper crowns and angel wings, sitting on bales of straw at the front. They had sung carols, done readings, acted out Nativity scenes – and the vicar had given them all a mince pie at the end. How could somewhere so friendly also feel so lifeless? In fact, how could any of this have happened?

Where were her mum and her baby sister, and why had

she left them alone? And her brother, where was he? They would all be in trouble.

Something made her turn around again and look out of the church door.

A noise, from the other side of the valley – a car horn, as a convoy of cars crossed the far hill, their headlights still shining bright in the early morning. Was it a search party? But they were driving in the wrong direction. Everything about this was wrong, in fact. They had crashed miles from where they were meant to be. So anyone looking for them was also bound to be looking in the wrong place. She tried to wave, but it was no good. They would never see her from this far away.

The cars didn't stop.

But, staring after them, she saw something far ahead, along the ridge from the church. There were black rocks and snow-capped telegraph poles and moving bits of white that could be sheep or toppling drifts or her frazzled mind – but there – was it possible? By that large tree. A moving object that wasn't a piece of the land or a creature that lived out there.

It was hard to see clearly in the dazzling morning light, but there was movement beneath the stark leafless spread of the tree. He was faint and far away, not much more than a dot from up here, but — it was a dot she recognised, an outline she knew all too well.

She turned away from the church and, yelling his name into the gathering winds, started to run.

When Mouse finally returned from the Wizard's Cave to the tree at the bottom of the cliff, the camp by the castle had changed.

In a large clearing, carpenters in rough tunics were hammering in a very long fence. It was a strange barrier, running straight down the middle of the field, with nothing at either end. And to the side more joiners were erecting a tiered stand of seats. For people to watch a fence? That seemed unlikely.

Mouse's heart leaped into his mouth as he realised.

It was a life-size replica of Junior Joust. Only it looked different in real life – so much bigger, rougher and . . . scarier. The fence was the tilt, to separate the knights as they parried. And the seats were for the audience who were going to watch him either triumph or fail. He had never had an audience for his jousting before. Mum did always say, 'Well done, lovely, that's brilliant,' when he reached a new level, but he wasn't sure whether she really got it. Violet thought it was silly, and Esme had no idea what the game even meant. She just loved to snatch it from him and change the settings. That drove him crazy. Speaking of his mum and his sisters, where were they? He wouldn't want them to miss this.

Then, as if a bony hand had stretched out of the fog, right through his back, and grabbed his heart, he stumbled.

For the first time, he remembered their names – and who they were.

And he missed them. He missed them more than he could ever have imagined. His sisters. The people he knew better than anyone else in the world. The games, the jokes, even the rows. Always being together at this time of year.

Where had they got to? They wouldn't want to miss his moment of glory. Mouse turned around, and the Junior Joust scenery disappeared. He was alone at the bottom of a steep hill, the snow getting in his eyes, with only his own footprints for company. There was no sign of his family, or anyone at all in fact.

His shoulders began to sink.

He couldn't do this. He couldn't walk another step.

Not in this cold. Not without the help of Vi or Esme.

But before he could dwell on his missing family any longer, a horse snorted in his ear.

'Nice of you to show up.'

'Nonky!' Mouse swung round and gave the horse a huge hug, suddenly realising how much he had missed his friends. And the Junior Joust scenery – the tilt, the crowds, and the tents – was back too, in full Technicolor.

'Hey – look but don't touch, please,' tutted Nonky. 'You think this braiding comes cheap?'

'I'm sorry,' said Mouse automatically, although he didn't really mean it. 'But you'll never guess where I've been. I ran away because I was frightened and didn't want you to see, but this talking owl rescued me – only he wasn't an owl, he was a wizard, and he could make food dance and transform himself into anything he wanted, and . . .'

He stopped, realising that everyone was looking at him oddly. Nonky's eyes were downcast, her expression unreadable. Sir Dragnet sat cross-legged on the ground, miserably twiddling the ends of his moustache, while Trex pretended to be flossing his tail spikes with a long line of bunting. Bar had her rear turned to him – never a nice sight – and was bleating quietly in a don't-mind-me kind of a way.

'What?' said Mouse. 'What is it?'

Everyone looked at their hoofs, or toes, or claws.

'Listen, you don't need to worry. It's going to be OK. The fight's going to be fine. I can do it. I can get us to the castle. I'm not scared any more.' Mouse found his throat going tight as he said the last words, and yet he didn't know why. Was that really true? That he wasn't scared any more? 'Well, I'm definitely not scared of you scaredy-cats or what you think,' he added.

As he said this, Mouse saw Trex miserably shrink a bit smaller in response, and he felt furious all of a sudden. 'What is everyone so sad about? We're going to win! I'm trying to tell you: I can make anything up!'

Sir Dragnet looked at the horse. 'Are you going to tell him or shall I?'

'Oh, sure, because I *never* have to give the bad news,' Nonky sighed.

'Wait. What bad news?' said Mouse.

Trex picked at his teeth with his claws. 'I dogh kno nugging,' he muttered. 'I jugh a dupid digosaur.'

'Well. No surprises there,' said the minstrel. 'I mean,' he mused, stroking his chin, 'I could always put it as a—'

'NO!' chorused everybody, including the carpenters

working in the field, who had never even met the minstrel before. Which is when all eyes fell on Bar, who was trying to make herself look as small as possible, hiding behind the others. This was quite difficult for a sheep of her size.

'Baa, baa, baa, baa, baa,' she was muttering, in an I'm-not-listening kind of a way, her head down close to the ground. But Mouse pushed through them all, treading on the dinosaur's tail and shoving Dragnet aside.

'Bar,' he said.

She looked straight up at him, her mouth full of soggy grass, and gulped guiltily.

'You have to tell me, Bar. Please. You woke me up. You're the one who brought me into this world. Tell me what is going on.'

'Baa,' she said in a why-is-it-always-sheep-who-have-to-do-the-heavy-lifting-at-times-like-this kind of a way.

'What is it, Bar?' asked Mouse.

'Baa,' said the sheep, in a this-only-making-one-sound-thing-is-really-challenging-my-ability-to-communicate-effectively kind of a way.

'Well, why don't you show me instead?' he said. 'You silly sheep,' he added softly under his breath.

Bar nodded, gritted her teeth and turned around. She was facing the horse's bottom. So she turned a little further, and found herself facing the wall of the tent. Finally, she turned one last time and began to waddle off through the camp.

Mouse set off after her as she waddled to the armourer's tent, where an amazing suit of polished steel was being banged into shape by a bearded blacksmith in a leather apron. He peered round the entrance to the tent, choking on the fumes oozing from the forge, the heat of the brazier scalding his eyes.

The armour was boy-sized. A boy-sized helmet, gleaming breastplate, thigh guards and elbow protectors.

'Is that for me?' Mouse asked in wonder, but the blacksmith just grunted and bent to his work with another echoing clang.

Then Bar was off again.

She wove between the crowds, which were growing in number all the time, munching on their pies and drinking out of clay pots, until he found her behind the city of tents. Here two serfs were lathing, showering up a blizzard of shavings, which covered the ground like woody snow. The thing they were working on, stretched over two trestles, was beautiful.

A lance.

Not just any old lance, but five pointy metres of glorious

red-and-white check. The weapon reminded Mouse of a football strip, a racing car and a space rocket all rolled into one. It made him feel excited and sick with nerves.

Before he could stay and admire the burnished point any longer, Bar was off again. She showed him seamstresses weaving braids of chequered silk and embroidering a scarlet surcoat with ermine trim. Next they inspected the training ground, where children were already riding wooden horses on wheels and bashing their blunt lances against a heavy bag of sand dangling from a branch.

He would have liked to watch the apprentice jousters and study their technique more closely: how they held their bodies and aimed their weapons and the exact moment in the charge that they struck the target, but there wasn't time because Bar was off again, this time to show him a swordsmith who was polishing swords much bigger and heavier than Wenceslas. Mouse was getting out of breath, trying to keep up with her through the jostling crowds.

'Bar! Stop!' he called, yet still the sheep trundled on.

And he began to realise why. All these things she was showing him were exciting and reassuring in equal measure. His colours were red and white, his lance was brand new and perhaps he would get a chance to practise

247

before the big event. It was all good to know, but none of it explained why his friends were so gloomy.

There had to be another reason. A reason the sheep didn't want to tell him.

That was it!

She was distracting him. She wasn't showing him anything sad or depressing. But she needn't have bothered. The wizard had made him decide he wasn't going to be afraid any more. This was all in his head. How could he be frightened of anything that was just a figment of his own imagination?

They were fast reaching the far end of the tournament fairground. The colourful tents and stalls became more and more scarce. Bar circled and circled, before reluctantly coming to a halt. Her scrubby tail hung between her legs and she lowered her head, her horns looking dejected. The crowds had vanished, and although Mouse could still hear their excited shouts and chatter, they had faded to only a faint hum, punctuated by the muffled clunk of the pages in training.

Mouse edged towards the sheep, picking his way carefully through waste the fairgoers had left behind, a tide of shattered drinking jugs and chewed chicken bones. He shivered. The cold was at his back again. For a brief moment he had been warmed by the fierce heat of the blacksmith's forge, the cheer of the fairgoers and the flushed, excited faces of the young mock jousters. But now his teeth were chattering and his fingers were sore.

Bar looked grey.

'W-w-what is it?' Mouse stammered. He found it impossible to speak without shivering. That was new. 'Show me what you're s-s-scared of. Show me. I won't be scared. I can't be scared of my own th-th-oughts, can I?'

The sheep looked at him long and hard, her brown eyes welling up. And she moved to the side.

A fog was rolling along the ground, but behind her, peering through the gloom, Mouse could make out the posts and rail of another training ground like the one she had shown him before. Beyond, in the murk, he could hear the clash of steel. It wasn't the young pages having a play-fight.

'Is it my opponent?' he asked Bar. 'The king's challenger?'

'Baa,' she said, in a we-didn't-want-to-worry-you kind of a way.

'What's he like?'

She gave a small sheep sigh and gestured with her horns for him to take a closer look.

As he did, the cold squeezed tight around his chest, dusting his eyes and lips with frost, making it harder to see and open his mouth. But he could open his eyes just enough to see who his challenger was. A silhouette loomed out of the swirling clouds, astride a fearsome white destrier.

The outline of a figure he had hoped was still far behind him.

For there, slicing the air with the sharpest blade he had seen yet, the colour of his armour unmistakable even through the smog, was the most fearsome challenger the king could have chosen.

The Pink Knight.

The Pink Knight approached Mouse through the mist, which now seemed to be whirling snow rather than fog, and brandished his sword. Or was it his hand? He made a strange growling noise, and Mouse took a faltering step back.

'N-no,' he said. 'You're not r-r-real. You c-c-can't h-hurt me.'

He looked around to see if Bar was there, so she could prove his point, but she had vanished. So too had the tents, flags, stalls, tiltyard and everything else. There were no crowds, no Nonky or Dragnet, no Trex – and no castle on the cliff above.

Beyond the oak tree were just rocks, snowdrifts and a stone wall. Behind the stone wall was a hill that rose up near vertically. Someone had carved big rough steps into the rock slope, which were encrusted with snow, thick and crisp as cake icing. Wiping his frost-crusted eyes, Mouse could just see there was a house right at the top of the hill.

A house. Not a castle, an enchanted forest or a wizard's cave. The outline of a long bungalow, like an old sheep barn, with coloured lights twinkling under the drooping snow-covered eaves. There was a welcoming glow in the windows. It felt so very far away, and yet not as far as it could have been.

He looked down at the sodden robot pyjamas plastered to his skin, his skinny feet shivering in his wellies. His fingers were swollen and purple. He licked his chapped lips, which only made them worse. Where was he?

Still clutching the damp toys – his toy horse, plastic dinosaur and battered iPad – under his arm, he somehow found his way down the bumpy slope towards the wall. It was laced with barbed wire under the snow, but he no longer cared about stuff like that.

There was something about that house. He had seen it before.

On the other side of the wall, at the bottom of the hill, the Pink Knight was waiting, armoured legs planted wide apart, extending a frosted gauntlet to him.

'No,' murmured Mouse, as if he was half asleep.

'Yes,' said the knight.

'You are my enemy,' said Mouse, shrinking back.

'As long as you think that, you will never enter the castle,' said the knight, and leaning across the wire – which didn't even scratch his armour – hoisted him gently over the barbs to the first step.

The rescue party was not about to find him. The rescue party was tired and weather-beaten. The rescue party was – finally – listening to Gramps's suggestion that they were looking in the wrong place. Weary searchers, their faces pale and drawn, were clambering into their four-by-fours and churning up the snow as they tried to reverse out of the various remote spots they found themselves in. Someone turned on the radio, only to find a wall of Christmas music, which they turned off straight away. No one was in the mood.

In the front passenger seat of one of the vehicles sat a grim-faced Inspector Carter, staring blankly out of the window, his gloved hands gripping the clipboard wedged between his knees. In the back sat an exhausted Gramps, his glasses still on his head, his wife leaning on his shoulder as she tried to grab a minute or so of rest. Her sleeping hand clutched her daughter's beret as tightly as any child would a teddy bear. Gramps didn't say anything, but his silence reverberated around the jolting vehicle, giving off such angry waves of disappointment and disapproval that Inspector Carter felt obliged to defend himself.

'It's not what you think, doctor,' he said eventually. 'It's not like the old days. Everything needs to be by the book. How about the men and women out there? I'm responsible for them as well — I can't just send them haring over any snow-covered peak I fancy on a whim. Especially not in these conditions.'

He hugged the clipboard tighter to his chest.

'I understand perfectly well, old fruit,' was all Gramps said in reply, rubbing his eyes, trying to contain himself. 'It's just that, so far, your chaps haven't found so much as a stray welly.'

'Which is why we are now moving operations into the adjoining valley. I know you're worried, but chances are they are probably just caught in a snowdrift or something and sensibly staying put. Or someone has taken them in and the phone line is down. The mobile signal is non-existent in places — you know that. Even if they have had . . . an accident . . . they might just be keeping warm. Anyhow, we're all moving there right away. More people, more kit.

We'll find them. It's not too late, not at all.'

Gramps sighed but said nothing, which at the same time said everything.

For all of them, Christmas Day was here whether they liked it or not. It was here for the boy on the road, the girl on the hill, the mother and child in the car, and half of Carsell searching for them over the way – with permission or not. Christmas Day had arrived, and as it ran on, so did something else that none of them could ignore – even though it was now day, even though it was shining a kind of sun across the wintry wastes.

Pressing on the back of the young boy, as the road and house disappeared from view and he found himself opening a striped tent flap and stepping once more into a welcoming circle of his old friends, it was the enemy of all their hopes.

Time was running out. And it didn't care who was in its way.

Mouse stuck his head out of the tent. It must be Christmas Day already, he supposed. For the first time in his life, he felt a real longing for it. He wanted to rush to a brightly lit tree and rip open some presents, even if they were just books. He could have eaten a whole plate of dry turkey with burnt pudding for after. He would gladly believe in any old made-up story in the world, just so as long as it wasn't the one he was in right now. Just so long as it was one that made him feel happy and safe.

There was an eerie stillness over the whole tournament field. Flags on the tops of the pavilions fluttered in the gentle breeze. The stand itself was already brimming with spectators, a pale wash of blurred faces. In the bright sunlight he saw flashes of silver from a raised seat in the middle of the crowd and wondered, with a catch in his heart, if that was the king who had set this impossible challenge.

He didn't know who this king was, and he cared even less.

The only thing that mattered was defeating his challenger so he could enter the castle.

Only then, at last, would this long journey be over.

He stepped outside, feeling the damp grass beneath his bare feet, and sucked in a gasp of cold morning air, stinging the back of his throat. Cheers and applause rose up from the field as the crowd were entertained by an archery display, arrows thwacking into straw targets from impossible distances.

Knights in foot armour staged mock duels as a warm-up for the main event. Their swords were blunted and the fights were not meant to be real, but every dull clang sent a shiver down Mouse's spine, as if he could feel each one himself. Peter the Marshal umpired, riding up and down on his nag, who was brightly clad in a sky-blue cape for the occasion. Mouse was less interested in Peter's horse though than in the one a groom was bringing to him. As Nonky was led around the side of the striped tent, he gasped.

Never had he seen a more impressive or handsome

creature. She was covered from nose to tail in a curtain of beaten gold. As it flapped in the wind, he caught a glimpse of her polished armour beneath, like a flash of danger. Straw stuck out of the edges, where it had been stuffed for extra padding. The saddle on her back was freshly oiled and buffed, the empty stirrups dangling loosely either side.

Mouse stared at her.

The horse returned his gaze with her one eye through a silver ringlet. 'What? Is the gold too much? Does it clash with my mane?'

He smiled and shook his head.

'Well, what are you waiting for, little knight? Are you ready?'

What a question. Who could ever be ready for this, which felt like the defining moment of his life? Yes, he had played thousands of hours of Junior Joust, perfecting his pacing and lance aim. He knew that a solid body shot was what every knight strove for, to unhorse his opponent. Attacking the legs or arms might cause injury or deflect a blow, but was unlikely to unseat the rider. A strike to the head could be fatal, but was much harder to land. And if you lost your focus for a moment, you risked everything. Time and time again he had cantered his digital steed up by the tilt, waiting for his moment, but never delaying too long. He did not know much about the world, but he knew how to time and aim a lance blow.

But that was just a game, a preparation for the real thing.

He held out his arms obediently, as grooms came forward to slide his tailor-made breastplate over them, fastening the leather ties so tight across his back that he could hardly breathe. That was correct, Sir Dragnet assured him. 'Keep it tight, you'll be all right – that's my motto, sunshine. You can either not breathe now, or stop breathing for ever; that's your choice and no mistake.'

But that did not make the fact that he could now barely breathe any easier, as if his chest was bound tightly by iron hoops.

A loud cheer filled the air as one of the two duelling knights was sent flying by a decisive blow to his helmet. Two servants carrying a litter rushed on to bear him away. It must be like being hit in the head while wearing a bucket, Mouse pondered. Your ears would ring for days. He was sure Farouk would have something to say about helmets and the long-term effect on your brain, but he wasn't here.

The world went dark as the grooms slipped his own helmet over his head, and his vision was reduced to a single thin strip of light in a world of darkness. They helped him on to the back of the horse, and laid the lance as gently across his lap as if it had been a rug, not a weapon.

Mouse took a deep breath, and then signalled Nonky to slowly enter the arena. He was still learning to keep his balance with his sight so reduced, and her swaying didn't help. He tried to focus on the jangling of her jewelled bridle to keep his attention dead ahead, not letting himself be distracted by the sudden hush that fell over the stands as they marched past. It felt as if everyone there was holding their breath, not just him.

'This armour is so heavy, Nonky. I keep thinking I'm going to fall off,' he wheezed to the horse.

'Just sit up straight and don't let them know you're scared.'

Peter the Marshal cantered up alongside them, waving a chequered flag. 'Hold yourself there, knight,' he snapped, before wheeling round and racing off to the other end of the field.

But Mouse barely took in his words.

A voice was calling his name from the stand – a lone fan, cheering him on perhaps. He tried to block the distraction from his mind and focused instead on the lance lying across his lap. Five metres of solid wood emblazoned in red and white, narrowing to a sharp point that glinted in the sun. A lance of war, Dragnet had said, not of peace. A weapon that, were he to point it in the right place at the right moment, could not only unseat his opponent but make sure he never got up again.

He thought of the Pink Knight. It was strange, he had tried to help him earlier, but that must have been a trick to try to disarm him. He had seen what the knight could do. Who knew if he was, even now, preparing to unhinge his jaw-piece and let his beard do his work for him? (Although Peter the Marshal probably had a form that the knight would have to complete first.) The lone voice from the stand was more and more insistent, but he had to ride on; there was no time for any more distractions.

The marshal sidled up on his horse, his silk cloak draped around his shoulders, holding the reins in one hand, a parchment scroll in another. This he unfurled, while his horse stepped back and forth, and began to read. 'By order of His Most Royal Majesty of the Castle of all Understanding, I am obliged to make you aware of the rules of this tourney.' He coughed. 'Firstly. Definitions. 1.1. The terms applied in this agreement shall supersede all other terms hitherto agreed or constituted by any party. Definition 1.2. In this document, the word *knight* is taken to mean you, the end user of our jousting services, and not

261

any horseback rider in general—'

Nonky brayed. She brayed so loudly that some of the audience gasped.

'Can we not just skip to the bit where Mouse pretends he has read the Terms and Conditions and accepts the Rules of Engagement?'

'But he hasn't!' snapped Peter the Marshal, looking more and more like Mr Stanmore. 'He hasn't. He only just passed his SATs. He hasn't done his GCSEs. He hasn't done his A levels or an NVQ. How is he supposed to make anything of this life if he hasn't done any exams? This kingdom is all about tests. If you can't pass the test, you don't deserve to live.'

'We haven't got time for this,' said Nonky. And with one graceful swipe of her armoured, one-eyed head, she sent the marshal careering off his horse, his skinny legs kicking the air, parchment and hunting horn flying.

Landing on the ground in a tangled heap of glossy cloak, to hoots of laughter from the stand, he raised the horn to his lips and blew. He made a perfect sound. The blast echoed around the craggy valley, bouncing off the timber stands, the cliffs and the castle above. 'In that case,' he shouted, one hand just keeping his pillbox hat pressed on, 'I declare His Majesty's tourney open! May the best knight win. Only one may enter the castle.'

The spectators in the stands fell quiet as a solitary drummer began to tap out a march, echoed by the heavy hoofs of an enormous horse. The tilt itself shuddered as the Pink Knight's charger clomped into view. The knight sitting astride it, even at this distance, was no less terrifying. He was pink and livid as ever. And lying across his lap was a lance black as night. It almost seemed to curl and wisp at the tips, like it was smouldering.

Somewhere behind him Mouse could hear the faint strumming of a lute. Sir Dragnet Derek was singing him one last song as he prepared to do battle. Only this time it was less like a song, and more like a football chant. Bar was baaing along in time and skipping around to the beat.

Mouse! Mouse! You can do it! Go on, my son!
Nice one, Mouse, nice one, my boy!
His horse has one eye, he's only got one lance
So go on, my lords, let's give him a chance
Nice one, Mouse, nice one, my boy . . .

For the first time, Mouse realised who Sir Dragnet reminded him of – that voice, those awful jokes and songs. But he couldn't hear him all the way from Florida, could he? It didn't matter, because the minstrel was drowned out by the whole stadium taking up his chant, and thousands of spectators were soon singing, 'Nice one, Mouse, nice one, my boy.'

The only voice he couldn't hear was Trex's. In fact, where was Trex? He hadn't seen him all morning. Mouse shrugged. Perhaps it was all too much for him, or more likely he was taking a giant-dinosaur-sized nap.

Nonky twisted her head around at him.

'Are you ready?' she asked again. There was a softness in her voice that hadn't been there before. It wasn't like Nonky normally sounded. She was being kind and gentle.

Then she wasn't Nonky any more, but was so many people. She was Mum, Violet and Esme. She was all those he was doing this for. With the chill of an ice dagger going through his brain, he remembered where they were too.

It had happened on Christmas Eve. Mum had been driving them all over the moors to Granny and Gramps', like they did every year. He and his sisters had been arguing, over books and toys and the iPad. There had been an accident – he couldn't exactly remember it – and he had gone flying through a hole –

The others would still be in the car. They might be hurt; they would be cold, hungry and alone. What on earth was he doing here, playing a game? His family were in terrible danger. He had to go to them!

But there wasn't time to worry any more, because with another toot of his brassy horn, Peter the Marshal trotted forward on his horse and raised his flag.

It snapped once or twice in the bitter wind.

Mouse's eyes watered as he grappled with his helmet. He had to speak up, make an excuse, get out of this before it was too late –

'Knights rea-dy . . . !' hollered the marshal, in his best sergeant-major voice.

And, with a single word, he lowered the flag. 'Charge!'

The two knights began to race towards one another, their lances raised. It was so incredibly heavy that Mouse wasn't sure how much longer he could hold it up for. Nonky was pounding the earth like her hoofs were on fire, and they might have been, for the amount of steam fuming from her nostrils. The Pink Knight charged, looming closer and closer.

Mouse tried to focus. He tried to remember everything he had learned from Junior Joust.

He was making this up. It was all in his head. It was just a game.

Now he could see the stains and dents in his opponent's armour, as the Pink Knight raised the smoking black lance towards him –

And Mouse thrust the red-and-white chequered pole with all his might across the tilt.

There was a satisfying crack and the sound of splintering wood as he and Nonky sailed past their enemy. Cheers rose up from the stands either side of them. He looked down at his lance, which was split and missing the tip, but otherwise in one piece. He turned around in his saddle and, to his dismay, saw the Pink Knight still mounted, trotting happily to the other end of the lists.

'Again! Again!' screeched Peter the Marshal. 'No score. No champion till we have a dismount.'

He waved his flag once more.

Nonky obediently turned and they began to charge down the line for a second time. Mouse was so weary. He tried to focus, to concentrate, but he was beginning to sweat inside the helmet, and his eyes were blurring.

There was a distant rumble from the stands, not like a crowd roaring though, something else. It didn't matter. He had to focus.

On came the Pink Knight, riding faster and harder than before –

As they drew level once again –

Mouse raised his splintered lance, and –

Nothing. No hit. Just air.

Instead, what he did feel was a sudden, sharp pain shooting across his breastplate, which made his whole body spasm.

A direct hit, like he was being gripped from the inside, his chest being squeezed between two iron-clad fists.

Where had all his breath gone?

He jerked, and toppled forward in his saddle.

Violet didn't care about the stitch tearing up her stomach, the spots flying before her eyes or the way the air scorched the back of her throat with every heaving breath. She cared about only one thing.

The oak tree, within sight now, the ridges of the bark coming into focus. Below it, across the field, was the boundary wall of Granny and Gramps's house, laced with barbed wire to stop sheep jumping over and getting at their garden. Although was that one there, trying to get in? She was more concerned by the figure who had climbed over the wall and was busy heaving himself up the broad stone steps that led up through the steep and unkempt slope of their back garden to Carsell Farm.

And then, right in front of her very eyes, he stopped.

Halfway up the flight of steps, he jerked, put his hand to his chest and crumpled to the ground, where he lay, not moving.

'Hang on, Mouse,' Violet cried. 'I'm coming!'

She hurtled towards the wall at the bottom of the slope. Here she found herself confronted by rows of wire, dusted with snow and flecked with chunks of sheep wool and a scrap of robot pyjama. With a hand so frozen it seemed more marble than flesh, she reached out and touched the piece of cloth.

'Mouse, have you gone crazy?' she wondered aloud. 'What kind of daydream were you having this time?'

She remembered she was meant to be crazy too. Gráinne O'Malley removed her woollen cape and laid it over the treacherous barbs, so she could clamber over the fence.

The relief of feeling some familiar ground under her feet for the first time since they had left the house the previous morning was tempered by the sight of a distant prone figure on the steps above. And beyond, at the summit, the warm glow of steamed-up windows, the twinkling lights of their grandparents' house.

It was going to be OK. She would tell Mouse not to worry any more, and would help him up, into her grandmother's arms, and all would be well. Then they would go back for Mum and Esme.

Mouse started with a blink. Nonky had sailed on, not realising for some moments that she was riderless. He could hear her returning, but it was too late. His enemy had vaulted off his horse. The Pink Knight unhinged his helmet and his beard began to spool out again, this time sharpening to a point. The point became a blade, which then sprouted a handle, carved in coils of clotted ink. He now brandished a terrifying new sword, as black as tar. Mouse's enemy stood astride him and with a roar raised this new weapon high above his head.

But Mouse was not done yet. He was not done at all. Drawing Wenceslas, he sprang to his feet and slashed at the Pink Knight, who deftly leaped to one side.

'You will have to try harder than that,' he grunted.

'I'm trying!' said Mouse, and lunged again with his lightsaber.

The knight shook his head, like he was sorry for something and, with a single blow of his enchanted black sword, shattered Wenceslas into a thousand pieces, showering like steel rain on to the ground.

'No!' said Mouse, and staggered back.

He was truly scared, more than he had ever been, fear rippling out from him in waves.

The rumbling he had heard from the stand earlier erupted into a roar that made the seating decks shake to their foundations. The crowd called out in confusion, before beginning to yell in panic as a shadow rose up over them. In among the screams, Mouse would have sworn he could hear someone calling his name.

But if they were, a roar from another creature obliterated their cry. Who could cast a stand holding thousands of people into darkness in the middle of the day? Who could block out the sun, so all that was visible was two burning red eyes in a black face? Who could smash the roof of the stand in half with a single blow of a clawed paw?

A dinosaur. A giant Tyrannosaurus rex, who had gorged on Mouse's fear, not to mention the fear of Bar, Sir Dragnet, Nonky and everyone watching his duel, as it went from bad to worse.

'Trex,' murmured Mouse, but there was little remaining of his toy in the monster towering above him. Meaty saliva dripped from the jaws in the sky as the spectators fled their seats, running for cover. Even the Pink Knight rested his sword for a moment, twisting his helmeted head up at the monster who blotted out the light.

Trex roared, and all the pretty banners blew over in a row of capsized sails. Mouse thought he heard, 'Shagh I each him?' from above, as the dinosaur waded through the stadium, the beams and awning ripped asunder as if they were matchsticks and tissue.

'Eat him!' yelled Mouse, clutching his chest. 'Eat him right up!'

He was surprised at how bloodthirsty he felt, and wondered if that was the right thing to feel, but he had no choice. Trex simply lifted one clawed foot over him and slammed it down in the turf next to the knight, who made no attempt to move or run away.

The dinosaur lowered his head and roared in the Pink Knight's face, a blast of hot air that accidentally sent Bar tumbling over and over, a giant bundle of wool blown away in a storm.

But the Pink Knight didn't flinch or bend.

He just stood still –

Trex ducked his head, and in a single mouthful –

With a sickening crunch of metal and helmet plume – he bit the knight's head clean off.

Silence fell across the field.

The dinosaur pulled back, chewing and swallowing, beginning to slowly shrink as everyone's fear lifted. And as the light returned, Mouse was shocked to see that the Pink Knight's body was still standing there, upright and stiff as a board. There was no shaking or blood spurting from his neck. Just a few wisps of smoke.

Who cared? The armour was obviously holding the

body up. His adversary was gone. The duel was won, with the help of his friends, and the castle would be his.

Mouse punched the air. 'Yes!' he screamed.

Sir Dragnet crawled out from the collapsed pie stall he had been hiding under, wiping some pastry crumbs from his moustache. 'Bravo, my lordling. I shall pen you a victory ode as soon as I can find a rhyme for tyrannosaurus.'

Bar picked herself up and began to trot back towards them, bleating happily in a well-if-that's-the-best-a-scary-knight-can-do-bring-it-on kind of a way. Only Nonky held back from congratulating her rider, her one eye frozen with unease.

To cheers and whoops from the crowd, Trex licked his lips and clapped his claws proudly. Mouse began to wrestle his helmet off, so he could go and give his most favourite dinosaur ever a hug, but as he did, something strange started to happen.

Trex began to hiccup.

At first it was just a small one. 'Excugh meagh,' he said, patting his chest.

Then it was a bigger one, and an even bigger one. They weren't just hiccups any more, but explosions coming out of his mouth.

With the hiccups, black smoke began to appear, curling

273

out of his nostrils and his ears and his eyes. The dinosaur burped, and clouds of the stuff billowed out. He took a couple of steps back with the shock, and came crashing down on the one surviving corner of the deserted and mangled seating stand, which collapsed beneath his weight.

Mouse and Nonky ran towards the fallen monster, who was convulsing and shaking, his belly pulsating with the worst case of dinosaur indigestion surely ever seen.

And, with one last horrific belch, Trex coughed something up.

It came shooting out of his mouth on a jet trail of smoke.

It soared high in the sky before plummeting down in front of Mouse, making a small crater in the green field. As the clouds cleared, as he coughed and spluttered with the fumes, Mouse saw what it was.

The head of the Pink Knight, still in its mangled helmet.

Before anyone could say or do anything, the Pink Knight's body walked calmly over, picked up the head and screwed it back on. It took a moment to twist into place, and he flexed his sword arm once or twice. Then he said, 'Where was I?' and began to swing his blade again at Mouse, who froze.

The once-mighty Trex was lying shrunken behind him, coughing and moaning to himself. The crowds and Peter the Marshal had long since fled. Sir Dragnet Derek, not renowned for his courage, was singing 'Nice One, Mouse' from his new hiding place behind Trex's tail – but so quietly, he needn't have bothered. Bar was in turn hiding behind him, making herself look as small as possible. Which was difficult. Only Nonky

275

stood her place, her one eye gleaming, her voice as calm as a lake.

'Like I said, kid, it's your story. Are you ready?'

And finally, he was.

He was not going to let this horrible, magic, evil, dinosaur-demolishing Pink Knight stand in his way.

The castle was just up there. It seemed to be closer somehow. He could see the golden drawbridge, the ghostly arrow slits and the ivory flags flapping in the air. He could smell the straw, taste the smoke from the kitchens and almost touch the silk banners draping the walls. He wasn't scared of anything any more. He accepted his fate.

As Violet scrambled up the hill towards him, she tried to call again, but she had shouted so much the whole night long she had almost no voice left. She watched in amazement as her brother heaved himself up out of the snow and began staggering up the last few steps. There was a large sheep stumbling after him too. It must have found a hole in the fence.

'No, you don't need to, Mouse!' she cried, but a gust of wind snatched her words cruelly away. 'Wait,' she said, her voice faltering. 'Help is coming. *I'm* coming.'

The gap between them was too far, too steep.

He was just a tottering dark figure in the twists of white above.

She tried again, putting her hands round her mouth, and screaming till she thought her vocal cords would snap. 'You don't need to rescue us any more. I'm here. Can't you see? Wait for me, and we can be brave together.'

Still the tiny figure stumbled on, as if powered by some other force, an energy she had never seen him driven by before.

'Oh, Mouse,' she said to herself, 'you silly little boy.' And she pictured herself sailing up towards him, navigating her faithful pirate craft through the wintry waves, driven by the wind, lifted by the sea, and guided by love.

All this she made herself imagine as she began to climb one last time.

There may be a castle. There was a castle, and he was going to get there, if it was the last thing he did.

The Pink Knight positioned himself at the end of the drawbridge, sword drawn, laughing.

Mouse flung himself at him. It hadn't been anyone's fault – it was just an accident. But he was going to put it right. He was going to get to the castle, and everything would be OK again for everyone.

He didn't care any more about the Pink Knight's beard, his sword or his stupid indestructible body. He cared about his mum, and making sure her presents got delivered on time. He wanted to see Violet's face when she discovered he had rescued them. And little Esme, covered with chocolate as she so often was.

He would wipe her clean himself.

Yes.

If he got through this, he would do everything to help everyone, all the time, every day. He would do anything, he swore. He would be helpful, extremely HELPFUL. He would even consider tidying his room. Anything to never see the Pink Knight again.

With a cry, Mouse brandished Wenceslas and hurled himself at the Pink Knight –

Violet stopped climbing the steps, heaving for breath. She could hear her brother screaming, but it sounded strong, like a warrior cry. And she could see now what he was holding . . . His lightsaber, waving it around and around. Why on earth . . . ? At whom? Not at the large sheep next to him, surely. And then she was screaming too.

Mouse closed his eyes, fearing the worst, the slice and the

stab. He muttered to himself, over and over again, 'I am not little, I am not scared, not of you, not of anything, any more, I will grow up, I am not little, I am not scared, you will let me into this castle . . .'

But the strangest thing happened. Or rather, didn't. There was no slice or stab. He dared to breathe again. His opponent's sword melted away, and Mouse found himself being enfolded in the knight's arms. They were heavy but felt soft.

The Pink Knight carried him over the drawbridge, and as he did, Mouse looked up at him, trembling with anger and fear.

'Who are you? You chased me all this way. Why? Why did you make me do this? Are you Death?'

The knight laughed, but in a nice way. He undid his helmet, and this time there was no toxic black beard, but only a warm shining face. 'Death did not make you do this. Did not, could not.'

'So are you God or something? I'm not religious, you know.'

'Nor am I a god. Just . . .' He bent down and whispered the word into Mouse's ear, who leaped out of his arms and ran towards the shimmering portcullis.

Mouse opened his eyes. They were stuck together with the cold and the wet and the wind, but he opened them anyway. He wanted to see inside the castle, all the finery and treasure and weapons, the kings and queens on their thrones. But there wasn't a castle. He turned around to ask the Pink Knight, but there was no Pink Knight either.

There was only a shape he dimly recognised, nearly falling over her frog-faced boots as she clambered towards him through the snow.

43

Mouse was expecting that the next thing he would do was enter the castle. He had been imagining what it would be like for so long.

He saw his scratched and dented armour transformed into a simple linen shirt and wool stockings, a single gold circlet about his head. The walls and pillars of the great hall would tremble as he walked past them, so delicate and fine he could almost put his hand straight through. Outstretched iron arms would brandish flaming torches on either side to welcome him, a velvet carpet would soften his footsteps, and scented air would blow gently across his skin. And everywhere he looked, somehow, he knew he would see other children – not just one or two, not even just hundreds, but thousands.

They were the children of war, of famine, of cruelty and neglect, and they were legion. And as Mouse saw himself entering, as one they raised their eyes and opened their mouths. They were so many it was hard to hear at first, but Mouse slowly realised it was the same word the Pink Knight had whispered in his ear as he carried him over the drawbridge.

But that wasn't what happened. Not at first.

Instead he went on another journey. Not like the journey he had made from the Haunted Forest to the castle, or even the one he now realised he had made from the site of the car crash to his grandparents' home. This was a different kind of trip, conducted at lightning speed.

It began with him sitting in a pushchair, blurred discs of light blaring towards him down the road, dazzling in the winter night. His mother was saying something to him, her hand resting on his shoulder.

Mouse realised that this was a memory, his first.

Next he was back at home, in East Burn, on a summer afternoon, the door to the garden lying open. His mother and Violet were outside, calling to him. Esme hadn't yet been born. And Mouse remembered this moment; he knew that this actually happened. Every detail felt so real – the

Velcro straps on his shoes, the itch of his sock against his calf, the smell of spring in the air.

He walked out over the step, on to the lawn, where there was a rug laid for a picnic. His mother was peeling an apple and patting the blanket, inviting him to join them.

'Look Mouse, it's such a beautiful day. We thought we'd have lunch outside – a home picnic. What do you think?'

He could hear the drone of bees on the lavender, which had never looked more purple. The sun shining so strongly that he had to shield his eyes. His sister laughing, and the grass soft beneath his feet. Up above his head, the clouds came and went in the sky.

And with them came so many other memories – at first, birthday cakes and songs, hats and candles.

Then, tumbling into his mind all in a rush: jumpers pulled over heads, muddy feet on bicycle pedals for the first time, or being dressed up as a sheep in white woolly tights for the school play. Now he was crouched in the boughs of a large tree, with Violet putting her finger to her lips. Or looking out of an aeroplane at the clouds below, the sky so pink beyond – followed by the taste of food in another country, so hot and different and unusual. Sunburn on his shoulders. The smell of after-sun lotion, pulling his first Christmas cracker, the plastic toy tumbling on to the floor . . . Crying in the school toilets for reasons since forgotten, and blowing his nose on paper roll . . . Unable to sleep one night, with a fever raging in his brain, Mum in the chair by the bed. That TV show! (And *that* one too.) The vivid colours on the screen, 3D on widescreen, popcorn on his lap . . . The sun catching ice on the frosted bathroom window, treading on a piece of Lego in bare feet, getting pins and needles from playing Minecraft for too long, a trip to London on a red bus and seeing where the queen lives, crunching autumn leaves underfoot and Dad swinging him in the air – just one more time – Mum reading that story, tucking him in, exchanging glances with Violet across the dinner table, Esme wearing that hat on her head which covered her eyes so she looked like a giant chicken and –

Mouse realised that, in all these moments, he was alive. He had been seeing, hearing, smelling, speaking, breathing and, quite ordinarily, joyously and unmistakably alive.

He had lived, he really had, and so he opened his eyes. He expected to be in the castle, surrounded by other children and wearing his linen and circlet of gold.

But he wasn't.

He was in a bed, wires sticking out of his arms, and a tube

in his nose. Everything was blurry at first, but the faces came into view. Mum. Violet. Esme was perched on Mum's lap, with Granny and Gramps sitting on the other side of the bed, holding hands. Behind Mum, a tanned but tired-looking Dad, wearing a very unChristmassy Hawaiian shirt.

A man in a shirt and tie with his sleeves rolled up was holding Mouse's wrist and shining a torch in his eyes. 'Hello, Mouse. We were just saying how brave you were. I had to explain to your mum that if you and Violet hadn't raised the alarm when you did, we wouldn't have found her and Esme in time. Such a brave boy . . . Mouse? Mouse? Can you hear me?'

Mouse smiled, and closed his eyes. He could hear a beeping noise, that grew louder and louder, until suddenly, it –

He opened his eyes again. Everyone had disappeared.

There in their place was Nonky, her armour more golden than ever, her one eye twinkling. Bar stood proudly alongside the horse, and it appeared that someone had managed to take a brush to her tangled curls, even if her horns were still wonky. Sitting on Nonky's back was Sir Dragnet, who had managed a change of outfit, into some very brightly-coloured minstrel clothes, perhaps the only ones in the Middle Ages to feature palm trees and sunsets.

Trex was quite a reasonable size and giving his very nicest bloodthirsty-dinosaur smile. He could see the wizard holding hands with what must be Mrs Wizard, and Peter the Marshal in a tie and shirtsleeves and filling in a form on a clipboard. The sun shone above them on the cliff-tops, and beyond was nothing but the endless blue sea.

And finally he knew, at long last, where the castle was.

It was all around, and always had been.

EPILOGUE

It would not be true to say that next Christmas was easy for the Mallorys. In fact, it was the hardest time they had ever shared together as a family. You would struggle to call it a Christmas at all. Everywhere Mrs Mallory looked, she saw him. Opening presents under the tree, yawning at lunch, skulking at the back of the post-dinner walk. She was keeping his room just as it was; to even think about tidying away a stray sock or stacking a single comic just broke her heart even more. His clean clothes stayed dry and neatly folded in the IKEA drawers. The robot pyjamas had been washed though, along with the Crocs. They had pride of place, in a small pile on top of the bed, along with a one-eyed toy horse and a plastic dinosaur.

Sometimes Violet pushed the door open an inch, to look

at the empty room and breathe in its scent. She hadn't known until this moment that nothing had its own smell, of nothingness. It was hard to describe, kind of flat and endless, a smell with no colour or depth. But it was strangely restful. Whenever she was sad or worried, Violet snuck into Mouse's room, pulling the door softly to behind her. Smoothing the faded duvet, she sat for a while on his bed and thought. She rested her chin on her hand and gazed out of the window. At the bare branches of winter, at the green buds of spring with their papery blossom swaying near to the glass, the dazzling light of summer, the layer of leaves drifting over autumn, and the little robin still pecking on the windowsill as the festive season came round again.

The season they all now liked the least.

As she stared, she wondered what Mouse would have said or done. If he would have even listened to her complaints or worries or silly stories, locked in his own world. But then she would have riled him, he would have reacted, there would have been jokes, maybe a fight – and everything would have been all right again until the next time. She smiled to herself in the glass as she realised she was daydreaming just as he once did, lost in a make-believe land beyond the clouds. As she looked down, the small mound of belongings came to remind her more and more of the wayside cairns they had noticed on their walks over the hills. Piles of stones to mark peaks, warn of pitfalls and highlight known paths. Sometimes even to offer remembrance, just like the special one they themselves had all made for him one chilly Sunday, across the valley, at the site of the crash. But more often than not, just to guide the way.

As Violet grew older, her legs longer, Mouse's bed seemed to shrink. How had her brother even fitted into such a tiny space? she wondered. Sometimes she didn't stroke the cairn of clothes and toys any more. Sometimes she dashed them to the floor. She was so cross with Mouse. The old questions felt as fresh in her mind as they had the day after. Why had he left the car and not stayed with them? Why had he gone? Until she would remember, with a flush of pride, what he had done, where he had gone for them.

Sometimes, when she was sitting on Mouse's bed, having these conversations with her absent brother, the door drifted open and her younger sister would watch her from the threshold, peeking through the gap and hoping her sister didn't notice her.

Esme watched her sister thinking about her brother.

A brother without whom she might not be here at all. Esme was jealous of Violet's connection and closeness, that she could have had too if he had lived, and angry with both her and Mouse that she couldn't share such a thing, but she had memories of her own. The brother she never really knew, whom she only remembered in flashes of colour and funny moments. As time passed these flashes became fainter, but she never forgot that there once had been a brother. And that he had adored her, played horsey games with her and always let her eat as much chocolate as she wanted.

None of these things made the next Christmas any easier, or the one after that.

Or indeed, Christmases many years after that.

And in fact, to the day that Mrs Mallory herself died, a happy great-grandmother, passing peacefully in her old bed at East Burn, surrounded by generations of Mallorys, photos of her parents and grandchildren and of her children including Mouse on the bedside table, she could never bring herself to love Christmas in the way she once had.

How could she?

But it got better.

Lots of things got better.

Violet grew up all the way and met a man called Tom

Smythe who wasn't scared of her (like all the others) but whom she loved as much as he loved her. Which was a great deal. They never had much money, but they were happy. Soon they had a baby, who made them even happier. A boy called Jack Mouse Mallory-Smythe. Jack was Violet and Tom's son, and he looked like them the most, but sometimes – when he turned his head and grinned, playing with toys on the floor – Violet saw someone else in his eyes, keeping a fond watch over her.

Esme was happy as a clam, married to Tess in America, teaching in a university. Right from a young age she had become fascinated, if not obsessed, with temperature. The temperature at which things freeze (or don't), the difference of degrees between life and death, and the effects extreme cold can have, not just on the body but the mind. She learned as much as she taught. Esme Mallory was never the kind to crow, but it wouldn't be an exaggeration to say that what she discovered about ice and snow would go on to change the way we all understand our own climate. Esme and Tess had a dog. A scruffy rescue terrier, who never did what she was told unless it involved making as much mess as possible. And this dog was called Nonky.

There were some things the Mallory family never talked about, couldn't talk about perhaps. Even as things got better, and the happier memories of Mouse largely replaced the sad ones. Things that remained unexplained. How had an eleven-year-old boy, dressed only in an anorak, robot pyjamas and wellies, managed to walk that distance, at night, in sub-zero temperatures, over such unforgiving countryside? The inquest summoned scientists and psychologists, who talked about the body's depths of stamina in such conditions. They talked about trances and fevers. Some even tested the soil by the old lead flue for psychotropic chemicals. Yet they never explained how Mouse appeared to have followed, buried under snow as it was, the path to his grandparents' house that he had previously only ever walked in the summer with his parents. Perhaps, it was suggested, he had followed the stray sheep with big horns who was found shivering next to him as he lay unconscious in the snow.

A few souls in Carsell, who had lived there even longer than Gramps had, muttered into their pints about the legends of the hills. The ancient tales about a mighty sorcerer buried under the mountain, waiting for his king to return, and take him to glory.

For some, the reason Mouse was able to make the journey he did that Christmas Eve was just a mystery. For others, it was a miracle.

But up on those old hills, which had lain there for millions of years, and were to lie there for millions of years more, there was no secret or mystery. There was only the wind, scuffing the rough grass, stones and trees, as it always had done. The wind stirred reeds, and rippled puddles. It combed sheep's fleeces, sometimes sending them to cower behind a wall. As the breeze blew across the land, it breathed the same word over and over again, so gently and so close to the ground that only those buried deep beneath the earth could hear. The word the Pink Knight had breathed into Mouse's ear on the drawbridge, the word that had welcomed him into the castle.

And the word was *imagine*. Just imagine.

ACKNOWLEDGEMENTS

It is not often that a book cover turns out to be exactly what one imagined while writing; for that happy turn of events I feel so lucky to have the fabulous Nicola Theobald once more as designer, with the mighty Rob Biddulph as illustrator – thank you both.

I am very grateful to Niamh Mulvey for her vital reading of the first draft, and to Talya Baker and Rachel Faulkner for their forensic scrutiny of the copy edit and proofs respectively.

This is my first book published with Quercus Children's in their new home at Hachette Children's Group, and I am very touched by the welcome and support from everyone there – Anne McNeil and Katy Cattell in particular.

If you read or heard about this book before you picked it up in a shop, that would have been down once more to the unstinting efforts of Lauren Woosey, Victoria Rontaler and Emily Thomas to whom all many thanks again for everything.

And always, I remain indebted to the three people whose great love, support, care and talent always makes anything I write so much better: my agent Clare Conville, my editor Sarah Lambert and my husband Will Tosh.

Join Kester on his animal adventures in the bestselling and award-winning

THE LAST WILD

trilogy

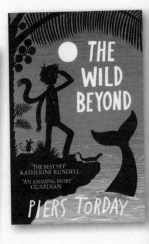

'An amazing story…
deserves to win prizes'
Guardian

'Inventive, with laughs,
tears and cliffhangers'
Sunday Times

'A wonderfully strange
and strangely wonderful book'
Financial Times

'Action-packed'
Daily Mail

'Written in a vivid, urgent style,
The Last Wild may be as critical to
the new generation as *Tarka the Otter*'
The Times

'Brings to mind the smarts
and silliness of Roald Dahl'
New York Post

WWW.PIERSTORDAY.CO.UK

Visit Piers for news,
school visits, events and more!